P9-CRG-895

Her small worries were forgotten

as she planned the garden. "Roses," she decided, "and lavender..."

Matilda had been talking to herself, something she quite often did, even if the cat wasn't there to listen. "It'll look lovely, I promise you."

She flung an arm wide and nearly fell over when the doctor said, an inch or so from her ear, "Do you often talk to yourself?"

She shot around to face him and he thought that she looked quite pretty with color in her cheeks and her hair hanging loose.

"I've never found the time," the doctor said mildly.

"Well, I don't suppose you would. Anyway, you would want to spend it with your f..."

She paused, not liking the cold look he gave her. She went on quickly, "Is it me you want to see about something?"

He was watching her idly. The shabby clothes she was wearing did nothing for her, but he had to admit that he liked her hair—and he was intrigued by her naturalness. Not his type, of course...

WHITE WEDDINGS

True love is worth waiting for...

Dear Reader,

Welcome to another book in our miniseries,
WHITE WEDDINGS.

Everyone loves a wedding, with all the excitement of the
big day: flowers, champagne and the thrill of the happy
couple exchanging vows....

In WHITE WEDDINGS you'll meet blushing brides and
gorgeous grooms, all with one thing in common: for better
or worse, they're determined the bride should wear white
on her wedding day...which means keeping passions in
check! Because for these couples, true love waits.

Happy Reading!

The Editors

Coming soon
The Faithful Bride
by
Rebecca Winters

Matilda's Wedding
Betty Neels

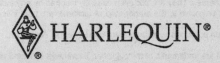

TORONTO • NEW YORK • LONDON
AMSTERDAM • PARIS • SYDNEY • HAMBURG
STOCKHOLM • ATHENS • TOKYO • MILAN • MADRID
PRAGUE • WARSAW • BUDAPEST • AUCKLAND

If you purchased this book without a cover you should be aware that this book is stolen property. It was reported as "unsold and destroyed" to the publisher, and neither the author nor the publisher has received any payment for this "stripped book."

ISBN 0-373-03601-9

MATILDA'S WEDDING

First North American Publication 2000.

Copyright © 2000 by Betty Neels.

All rights reserved. Except for use in any review, the reproduction or utilization of this work in whole or in part in any form by any electronic, mechanical or other means, now known or hereafter invented, including xerography, photocopying and recording, or in any information storage or retrieval system, is forbidden without the written permission of the publisher, Harlequin Enterprises Limited, 225 Duncan Mill Road, Don Mills, Ontario, Canada M3B 3K9.

All characters in this book have no existence outside the imagination of the author and have no relation whatsoever to anyone bearing the same name or names. They are not even distantly inspired by any individual known or unknown to the author, and all incidents are pure invention.

This edition published by arrangement with Harlequin Books S.A.

® and TM are trademarks of the publisher. Trademarks indicated with ® are registered in the United States Patent and Trademark Office, the Canadian Trade Marks Office and in other countries.

Visit us at www.romance.net

Printed in U.S.A.

CHAPTER ONE

DR LOVELL looked across his desk to the girl sitting in front of it. She would have to do, he supposed; none of the other applicants had been suitable. No one, of course, could replace the estimable Miss Brimble who had been with him for several years before leaving reluctantly to return home and nurse an aged parent, but this girl, with her mediocre features and quiet voice, was hardly likely to upset the even tenor of his life. There was nothing about her appearance to distract him from his work; her mousy hair was in a smooth French pleat, her small nose was discreetly powdered, and if she wore lipstick it wasn't evident. And her clothes were the kind which were never remembered... She was, in fact, suitable.

Matilda Paige, aware that she was being studied, watched the man on the other side of the desk in her turn. A very large man, in his thirties, she guessed. Handsome, with a commanding nose and a thin mouth and hooded eyes and dark hair streaked with silver. She had no intention of being intimidated by him but she thought that anyone timid might be. A calm, quiet girl by nature, she saw no reason to stand in awe of him. Besides, since the moment she had set eyes on him, not half an hour ago, she had fallen in love with him...

'You are prepared to start work on Monday, Miss Paige?'

Matilda said yes, of course, and wished that he would smile. Probably he was tired or hadn't had time for a proper breakfast that morning. That he had a good housekeeper she had already found out for herself, whose brother did the gardening and odd jobs. She had also discovered that he was engaged. A haughty piece, Mrs Simpkins at the village shop had said—been to stay accompanied by her brother once or twice, hadn't liked the village at all and said so.

'Rude,' Mrs Simpkins had said. 'Them as should know better should mind their manners; grumbled 'cos I didn't 'ave some fancy cheese they wanted. Well, what's good enough for the doctor should be good enough for them. 'E's a nice man, none better, just as 'is dad was a good man, too. A pity 'e ever took up with that young woman of 'is.'

Matilda, sitting primly on the other side of his desk, heartily agreed with Mrs Simpkins. All's fair in love, she reflected, and got up when he gave his watch a brief glance.

Dr Lovell got up too; his manners were nice... She bade him a brisk goodbye as he opened the surgery door for her and then, shepherded by his practice nurse, left the house.

It was a pleasant old house in the centre of the village. Queen Anne, red-bricked with massive iron railings protecting it from the narrow main street. Lovells had lived there for generations, she had been told, father passing on his profession to son, and this particular twentieth-century son was, from all accounts, acknowledged to be quite brilliant. He had refused offers of important posts in London and preferred to remain at his old home, working as a GP.

Matilda walked briskly down the street, smiling rather shyly at one or two of the passers-by, still feeling that she didn't belong. The village was a large one, deep in rural Somerset, and as yet had escaped the attention of developers wanting to buy land and build houses, probably because it lay well away from a main road, astride a tangle of narrow country lanes. Because of that, inhabitants of Much Winterlow were slow to accept newcomers. Not that there was anything about the Reverend Mr Paige, his wife and daughter to which they could take exception. Upon his retirement owing to ill health, her father had been offered by an old friend the tenancy of the small house at the very end of the village and he had accepted gratefully. After the rambling vicarage he had lived in for many years, he found the place cramped but the surroundings were delightful and quiet and he would be able to continue writing his book...

Matilda could see her new home now as she came to the end of the last of the cottages in the main street. There was a field or two, ploughed up in readiness for the spring next year, and the house, facing the road—square and hardly worth a second glance, built a hundred years or so earlier as home for the agent of the big estate close by and then later left empty, to be rented out from time to time. Her mother had burst into tears when she had first seen it but Matilda had pointed out that they were fortunate to have been offered it at a rent her father could afford. She'd added cheerfully, 'It may look like a brick box but there's no reason why we shouldn't have a pretty garden.'

Her mother had said coldly, 'You are always so sensible, Matilda.'

It was a good thing that she was, for her mother had no intention of making the best of a bad job; she had led a pleasant enough life where her husband had been rural dean; true, the house had been too big and if it hadn't been for Matilda living at home and taking most of the household chores onto her shoulders there would have been little time to play the role of vicar's wife. A role Mrs Paige had fulfilled very well, liking the social status it gave her in the small abbey town. But now she was forced to live in this village in a poky house with barely enough to live on...

Matilda pushed open the garden gate and went up the brick path to the front door. The garden was woefully neglected; she would be able to do something about that while the evenings were still light.

She opened the door, calling, 'It's me,' as she did so, and, since no one replied, opened the door on the left of the narrow hallway.

Her father was at his desk, writing, but he looked up as she went in.

'Matilda—it isn't lunchtime, surely? I am just about to...'

She dropped a kiss on his grey head. He was a mild-looking man, kind-hearted, devoted to his wife and to her, content with whatever life should offer him, unworried as to where the money would come from to pay their way. He hadn't wanted to retire but when it had become a vital necessity he had accepted the change in his circumstances with a good grace, accepted the offer of this house from an old friend and settled down happily enough to write.

That his wife was by no means as content as he was was a worry, but he assumed that, given time, she would settle down to their new life. Matilda had given him no worries; she had accepted everything without demur, only declaring that if possible she would find a job.

When she had left school she had taken a course in

shorthand and typing, learned how to use a computer and simple bookkeeping. She had never had the chance to use these skills, for her mother had needed her at home, but now, several years later, she was glad that she would be able to augment her father's pension. It had been a lucky chance that Mrs Simpkins had mentioned that the doctor needed a receptionist...

She left her father with the promise of bringing him a cup of coffee and went in search of her mother.

Mrs Paige was upstairs in her bedroom, sitting before her dressing table, peering at her face. She had been a pretty girl but the prettiness was marred by a discontented mouth and a frown. She turned away as Matilda went in.

'The nearest decent hairdresser is in Taunton—miles away. Whatever am I going to do?' She cast Matilda a cross look. 'It's all very well for you; you're such a plain girl, it doesn't really matter...'

Matilda sat down on the bed and looked at her mother; she loved her, of course, but there were times when she had to admit that she was selfish and spoilt. Hardly Mrs Paige's fault—she had been an only child of doting parents and her husband had indulged her every whim to the best of his ability and Matilda had been sent away to boarding-school so that she had never been close to her daughter.

And Matilda had accepted it all: her father's vague affection, her mother's lack of interest, her life at the vicarage, helping Sunday school, the Mother's Union, the annual bazaar, the whist drives... But now that was all over.

'I've got the job at the doctor's,' she said. 'Part-time, mornings and evenings, so I'll have plenty of time to do the housework.'

'How much is he paying you? I can't manage on your father's pension and I haven't a farthing myself.'

When Matilda told her she said, 'That's not much…'

'It's the going rate, Mother.'

'Oh, well, it will be better than nothing—and you won't need much for yourself.'

'No. Most of it must go for the housekeeping; there might be enough for you to have help in the house once or twice a week.'

'Well, if you are working for most of the day I shall need someone.' Her mother smiled suddenly. 'And poor little me? Am I to have something too? Just enough so that I can look like a rural dean's wife and not some poverty-stricken housewife.'

'Yes, Mother, we'll work something out without disturbing Father.'

'Splendid, dear.' Her mother was all smiles now. 'Let me have your wages each week and I'll see that they are put to good use.'

'I think I shall put them straight into Father's account at the bank and just keep out enough for you and me.'

Her mother turned back to the mirror. 'You always have been selfish, Matilda, wanting your own way. When I think of all I have done for you…'

Matilda had heard it all before. She said now, 'Don't worry, Mother, there will be enough over for you.'

She went across the small landing to her own room, where she sat down on her bed and did sums on the back of an envelope. She was well aware of the inadequacies of her father's pension; if they lived carefully there was just enough to live on and pay the bills; anything extra had to be paid for from his small capital—

smaller still now with the expense of his illness and their move.

He had received a cheque from his parishioners when he had left the vicarage, but a good deal of that had been swallowed up by carpets and curtains and having the functional bathroom turned into one in which Mrs Paige could bear to be in. The bathroom as it was had been adequate, but her father loved his wife, could see no fault in her, and since she'd wanted a new bathroom she had had it...

He was an unworldly man, content with his lot, seeing only the best in other people; he was also impractical, forgetful and a dreamer, never happier than when he could sit quietly with his books or writing. Matilda loved him dearly and, although his heart attack had led to his retirement and coming to live in straitened circumstances, she had welcomed it since it meant that he could live a quiet life. Now she had a job and could help financially she had no doubt that once her mother had got over her disappointment they would be happy enough.

She went downstairs to the small kitchen to make coffee, and while the kettle boiled she looked round her. It was a rather bare room with an old-fashioned dresser against one wall, an elderly gas cooker and the new washing machine her mother had insisted on. The table in its centre was solid and square—they had brought it with them from the vicarage—and there were four ladder-backed chairs round it. By the small window was a shabby armchair, occupied by the family cat, Rastus. Once she had a little money, decided Matilda, she would paint the walls a pale sunshine-yellow, and a pretty tablecloth and a bowl of bulbs would work wonders...

She carried the coffee into the living room and found her mother there. 'I'll take Father his,' Matilda suggested, and she crossed the hall to the small, rather dark room behind the kitchen, rather grandly called the study. It was very untidy, with piles of books on the floor awaiting bookshelves, and more books scattered on the desk, which was too large for the room but Mr Paige had worked at it almost all of his life and it was unthinkable to get rid of it.

He looked up as she went in. 'Matilda? Ah, coffee. Thank you, my dear.' He took off his spectacles. 'You went out this morning?'

'Yes, Father, for an interview with Lovell who has the practice here. I'm going to work for him part-time.'

'Good, good; you will meet some young people and get some sort of a social life, I dare say. It will not entail too much hard work?'

'No, no. Just seeing to patients and their notes and writing letters. I shall enjoy it.'

'And of course you will be paid; you must get yourself some pretty things, my dear.'

She glanced down at the desk; the gas bill was lying on it and there was a reminder from the plumber that the kitchen taps had been attended to.

'Oh, I shall, Father,' she said in an over-bright voice.

On Monday morning Matilda got up earlier than usual, took tea to her parents and retired to her room. She couldn't turn herself into a beauty but at least she could be immaculate. She studied her face as she powdered it and put on some lipstick. She wiped it off again, though. She hadn't worn it at the interview, and although she didn't think that Dr Lovell had noticed her at all there was always the chance that he had. She suspected that she had got the job because she was as near alike to Miss Brimble as her youth allowed.

She had met that lady once: plain, bespectacled, clad in something dust-coloured. There had been nothing about her to distract the eye of Dr Lovell, and Matilda, unable to find anything in her wardrobe of that dreary colour, had prudently chosen navy blue with a prim white collar. Such a pity, she reflected, dragging her hair back into its French pleat, that circumstances forced her to make the least of herself.

She pulled a face at her reflection. Not that it mattered. She had as much chance of attracting him as the proverbial pig had of flying. Falling in love with a man who hadn't even looked at you for more than a moment had been a stupid thing to do.

The surgery was at one side of the house and a narrow path led to the side door. It was already unlocked when she got there and a woman was dusting the row of chairs. Matilda bade her good morning and, obeying the instructions she had been given, went into the surgery beyond. The doctor wasn't there; she hadn't expected him to be for it was not yet eight o'clock.

She opened a window, checked the desk to make sure that there was all that he might need there, and went back to the waiting room where her desk stood in one corner. The appointments book was on it—he must have put it there ready for her and she set to, collecting patients' notes from the filing cabinet by the desk. She had arranged them to her satisfaction when the first patient arrived—old Mr Trimble, the pub owner's father. He was a silent man with a nasty cough and, from his copious notes, a frequent visitor to the surgery. He grunted a greeting and sat down, to be joined presently by a young woman with a baby.

Neither the mother nor the baby looked well, and Matilda wondered which one was the patient.

The room filled up then and she was kept busy, aware of the curious looks and whispers. Miss Brimble had been there for so many years that a newcomer was a bit of a novelty and perhaps not very welcome.

Dr Lovell opened his surgery door then, bade everyone a brisk good morning, took Mr Trimble's notes from Matilda and ushered his patient inside. He ushered him out again after ten minutes, took the next lot of notes from her and left her to deal with Mr Trimble's next appointment.

It wasn't hard work but she was kept busy, for the phone rang from time to time, and some of the patients took their time deciding whether the appointments offered them were convenient, but by the time the last person had gone into the surgery Matilda was quite enjoying herself. True, Dr Lovell had taken no notice of her at all, but at least she'd had glimpses of him from time to time...

She dealt patiently with the elderly woman who was the last to go for she was rather deaf and, moreover, worried about catching the local bus.

'My cats,' she explained. 'I don't like to leave them for more than an hour or two.'

'Oh, I know how you feel,' said Matilda. 'I have a cat; he's called Rastus...'

The door behind her opened and Dr Lovell said, with well-concealed impatience, 'Miss Paige...'

She turned and smiled at him. 'Mrs Trim has a cat, and so have I. We were just having a chat about them.'

She bade Mrs Trim goodbye, shut the door behind her and said cheerfully, 'I'll tidy up, shall I?'

He didn't answer, merely stood aside for her to fol-

low him back into the surgery. As they went in, the
door leading to the house opened and a tall, bony
woman came in with a tray of coffee.

Matilda bade her good morning. 'How nice—coffee,
and it smells delicious.'

The doctor eyed her with an inscrutable face.
Matilda had seemed so meek and quiet during her interview. He said firmly, 'While you drink your coffee,
please make a note of various instructions I wish to
give you.'

She didn't need to look at him to know that she had
annoyed him. She said, 'I talk too much,' and opened
her notebook, her nose quivering a bit at the aroma
from the coffee pot.

'Be good enough to pour our coffee, Miss Paige. I
should point out that, more frequently than not, you
may not have time for coffee. This morning was a very
small surgery and normally I depart the moment the
last patient has gone, leaving you to clear up and lock
the door and the cabinets. I should warn you that the
evening surgery is almost always busy.'

He opened a drawer and handed her a small bunch
of keys. 'If I am held up then I rely upon you to admit
the patients and have everything ready, or as ready as
possible, for me. Miss Brimble was most efficient; I
hope that you will be the same.'

Matilda took a sip of coffee. Strange, she mused,
that, of all the millions of men in the world, she should
have fallen in love with this coldly polite man with
cold blue eyes and, for all she knew, a cold heart as
well.

'I shall do my best to be as like Miss Brimble as
possible,' she told him, and after he had given her a
list of instructions she asked, 'Do you want me for

anything else, Doctor? Then I'll just tidy the waiting room and lock up.'

He nodded, not looking up from the pile of notes on his desk. 'I shall see you this evening, Miss Paige.' He glanced up then. 'This is not a job where one can watch the clock too closely.'

She got up and went to the door, where she said in a quiet little voice, 'I expect you miss Miss Brimble. We must hope for the best, mustn't we?'

She closed the door quietly behind her and the doctor stared at it, surprise on his handsome face. But presently he allowed himself to smile. Only fleetingly, though. Miss Paige must conform to his ways or find another job.

Matilda went home, donned an apron and began to load the washing machine. Her father was in the study; her mother was getting coffee in the kitchen.

'Well, how did you get on?' she asked. 'I don't suppose it was hard work. Is he nice? Your father has to see him within the next few days. Such a nuisance that he has to see the doctor so often; I should have thought that once he had got over his heart attack he would have been cured.'

'Well, he is cured, Mother, but it's possible to have another attack unless a doctor keeps an eye on him. He's feeling fine, though, isn't he? This is the ideal life for him…'

Mrs Paige said fiercely, 'Oh, it's perfect for him but what about me? There's nothing to do here in this poky little village…'

'It's not poky. It's really quite large and Mrs Simpkins was telling me that there's always something going on. There's amateur theatricals in the winter, and bridge parties, and tennis in the summer and cricket. Once you get to know the people living here—'

'And how do I do that? Knock on people's doors? We've been here almost two weeks.'

'If you went to the village more often...' began Matilda. 'Everyone goes to the village shop...'

'Everyone? Who's everyone? No one I can make a friend of. When I think of the pleasant life we had at the vicarage—my friends, the interesting people who came to see your father...'

'I'm sure there are interesting people here, too,' said Matilda. 'Are you going to have coffee with Father? I had some at the surgery. Shall I make a macaroni cheese for lunch?'

Her mother shrugged. 'What is he like? Dr Lovell? A typical country GP, I suppose.'

Matilda didn't answer that; she didn't think that Dr Lovell was typical of anyone, but then, of course, she was in love with him.

She took care to be at the surgery well before five o'clock. She had the patients' notes ready on his desk and was sitting at her own desk in the waiting room when the first patient arrived. The doctor had been right; there was a steady stream of patients—several nasty coughs, a clutch of peevish children and two young men with bandaged hands. She had seen from the notes that most of them had come from outlying farms, and since they all appeared to know each other the room was full of cheerful voices interspersed with coughing fits and whining small voices.

There was no sign of the doctor and it was already well after five o'clock. Matilda left her desk to hold a fractious toddler while its mother took an older child to the loo. She was still holding it when the surgery door opened and the doctor invited his first patient, an old man with a cough, to come into the surgery.

He looked at Matilda with raised eyebrows but made no comment and by the time he called for his second patient she was back at her desk, busy with the appointments book, very aware that she was being looked over by everyone there. After all, she was a newcomer to the village, and although Mrs Simpkins had given her opinion that Matilda was a nice young lady—a bit quiet, like, but polite—the village had no intention of making up its mind in a hurry.

Parson's daughter, they told each other—well, Miss Brimble had been that, too, but twice this one's age. They bade her a lot of cheerful good evenings as they went home and over their suppers gave their varied opinions: a nice enough young lady, not much to look at but with a ready smile.

As for the doctor, dining at the Reverend Mr Milton's table that evening, he professed himself satisfied with his new receptionist. He had no more to say about her than that, though.

The week progressed. Tuesday was an evening surgery only for he held the post of anaesthetist at Taunton Hospital and spent the day there. On Wednesday the surgery bulged with victims of the first serious chills of winter and on Thursday there was no surgery in the evening. Matilda enjoyed her work although she wished it could have been conducted in a clearer atmosphere than the surgery, redolent of damp coats and the earthy smells clinging to farm workers who came in straight from their work. But she had found her sensible feet by now and she was happy despite the doctor's chilly politeness towards her. At least she saw him each day and sooner or later he would stop comparing her with Miss Brimble and decide that she was quite nice, really...

And, Matilda being Matilda, she already had a few plans. A potted plant for the waiting room, a small vase of flowers for the doctor's desk, a chamber pot for the small children—she wondered why Miss Brimble hadn't thought of that—and some container where people could put their dripping umbrellas. There were still a lot of odds and ends her mother had consigned to the garden shed; there might be something suitable there...

After the first morning she had politely refused coffee after the morning surgery, standing by his desk, listening to whatever it was he needed to tell her and then bidding him a cheerful good morning, shutting the door quietly behind her.

There was no point in sitting there drinking coffee when he was so obviously unaware of her. She would then tidy the waiting room, lock up and go home.

There was an envelope on her desk on Friday morning. She had asked at her interview if she could be paid each week and in cash, and he had agreed without comment. She put it in her handbag and bade the first patient good morning. Her father had taught her that money was no easy path to happiness but she couldn't help feeling rich...

There was a small branch of her father's bank in the village, open on three days a week for a few hours. Matilda paid most of the money into his account, bought sausages from Mrs Simpkins and went home, treading on air.

There was a car parked outside the gate when she reached it: an elderly Rover, immaculately kept. It belonged to the Reverend Mr Milton and she was pleased to see it for it meant that that gentleman had come to

visit her parents. He had called briefly a day or so after
they had moved in but the place had been in chaos and
he hadn't stayed.

He was in the living room and his wife was with
him. Mrs Milton was a small, placid lady with a kind
face, and according to Mrs Simpkins was very well
liked in the village.

Matilda shook hands and, bidden by her mother,
went to fetch more coffee, sorry that she hadn't brought
some biscuits with her. She handed around second cups
and sat down to answer Mrs Milton's gentle questions.

She liked her job with Dr Lovell? Such a dear, good
man but very overworked; so fortunate that he had
found Matilda to replace Miss Brimble. And did
Matilda play tennis? In the summer there was a flour-
ishing club—and amateur theatricals in the winter.
'You must meet some of the younger ones here,' said
Mrs Milton.

Mrs Paige interrupted her in the nicest possible way.
'Matilda isn't a very sociable girl,' she said. 'Quite a
homebird in fact, which is so fortunate for I'm not very
strong and all the worry of my husband's illness has
upset my nerves.'

Mrs Milton said that she was sorry to hear it. 'I was
hoping you would enjoy meeting a few people here and
perhaps join me on one or two of our committees. We
do a good deal for charity in a quiet way. And the
Mother's Union flourishes. Lady Truscott is our pres-
ident and we meet each month at her house. The
Manor, you know...'

'I shall be delighted to do that and give what help I
can.' Mrs Paige had become quite animated. 'And anything else that I can do in my small way.' She gave a
rueful little laugh. 'This is all so strange. And I do miss

the house—and the social life attached to the church. And, of course, the ease with which one could obtain things. It seems I must go all the way to Taunton to a hairdresser.'

'There's Miss Wright in the village; she is really not at all bad. I must confess that I go to Tessa's in Taunton. If you would like it I'll give you her phone number and if you mention my name I'm sure she will fit you in.'

'That's most kind. It would have to be on the day the bus goes to Taunton; I'm told that there is one.'

'You don't drive?'

'No, unfortunately not, and, of course, Jeffrey isn't allowed to, so we sold the car.'

Mrs Milton turned to Matilda. 'You don't drive, my dear?'

Matilda just had time to say yes, before her mother said quickly, 'There seemed no point in keeping the car just for Matilda's use. She enjoys walking and there is a bicycle she can use.'

'In that case,' said Mrs Milton, 'I'll be glad to offer you a lift the next time I go to Taunton. Matilda, too…'

'One of us has to stay home just in case Jeffrey isn't well, but I'd be glad of a lift; it's most kind of you to offer. Perhaps I could fit it in with the hairdresser and have time for a quick shop. I'm sure the shop in the village is excellent but there are several things I need which I'm sure aren't stocked there.'

'We will arrange something soon and I'll let you know about joining our committee.' Mrs Milton got to her feet. 'I'm glad you have come here to live and I'm sure you will be happy once you have settled in.'

She caught her husband's eye and he rose reluctantly from the earnest talk he was enjoying with Mr Paige.

Goodbyes were said and Matilda saw them out of the gate and into their car, waving them away with a friendly hand.

'A very nice girl,' said Mrs Milton, 'but I don't imagine she has much of a life. Her mother…'

'Now, my dear, don't be too hasty in your judgement, although I do see what you mean. We must endeavour to find Matilda some friends.'

'I wonder how she gets on with Henry?'

'Presumably well enough; I don't imagine he's a hard taskmaster. Once they have got used to each other I'm sure she will prove every bit as efficient as Miss Brimble.'

Which wasn't what Mrs Milton had meant at all, although she didn't say so.

Mrs Paige followed Matilda into the kitchen. 'Did you get paid?'

Matilda stacked cups and saucers by the sink. 'Yes, Mother.'

'Good. If Mrs Milton phones I can go to Taunton. I need one or two things as well as having my hair done. If you'd let me have twenty-five pounds? You must see that if I'm to meet all these women I must look my best, and you'll have the rest of your money…'

'I've paid it into Father's account at the bank.'

'Matilda—are you out of your mind? His pension will be paid in in a week or so and we can open an account at the shop.'

'There's a gas bill overdue and the plumber to be paid…'

Mrs Paige said tearfully, 'I can't believe that my own daughter could be so mean.' She started to cry. 'I hate it here; can't you understand that? This poky little house and no shops and nothing to do all day. There was always something at the vicarage—people calling, wanting advice or help; things happening.' She added, 'Of course you don't care; I don't suppose you miss your friends and it isn't as if there were any men keen on you. It's just as well, for I doubt if you'll meet anyone here who'll want to marry you.'

Matilda said quietly, 'No, I don't suppose I will. I'm sorry you're unhappy, Mother, but perhaps you will meet some people you will like when you see Mrs Milton again.'

She took some notes out of her handbag. 'Here is twenty-five pounds.' She laid the money on the table. 'I'll get lunch, shall I?'

Her mother said something but she didn't hear it, for she was fighting a strong wish to run out of the house, go somewhere where she wasn't reminded that she was dull and plain and mean. Life would have been so different if she had been pretty...

She gave herself a shake. Self-pity was a waste of time; and life wasn't all that bad. She had a job, she liked the village and the people she had met were friendly, and there was Dr Lovell. If they hadn't come here to live she would never have met him. The fact that he didn't like her overmuch made no difference to the fact that she was in love with him. That coloured her dull days and perhaps in time, if she could be more like Miss Brimble, he would like her after all. She didn't expect more than that; her mother had made it plain that there was nothing about her to attract a man such as he.

She got the lunch, listened to her father's cheerful comments about their visitors and her mother's plans to go to Taunton and then, with Rastus for company,

Matilda went into the garden. It had once been very pretty but was now woefully overgrown. She began raking the leaves which covered the patch of grass in front of the house.

It was chilly and there was a fresh wind, so that her hair blew free from its tidy pleat, and she had tied a sack over her skirt. The doctor, driving past, thought she looked very untidy, obviously not bothering about her appearance. He dismissed her from his mind and was vaguely irritated to find himself remembering all that pale brown hair, tossed about by the wind.

CHAPTER TWO

THERE was nothing about Matilda's appearance on Monday morning to remind him of her scruffy appearance in the garden. The picture of neatness, she dealt with the patients with good-humoured patience and real pleasure, for she felt that she had been accepted by the village, included in their gossip as they waited their turn. It was to be hoped, she reflected, that Dr Lovell would accept her, too...

It was a chilly, drizzly morning and she was glad that she had lugged the chimney pot she had found in the garden shed down to the doctor's house and installed it in the waiting room. It wasn't ideal but at least it was somewhere to put the umbrellas. She was sure that the doctor hadn't noticed it; hopefully he wouldn't notice if she brought some of the neglected chrysanthemums from the back garden and put them on the table in the waiting room—and on his desk; they might cheer him up...!

The surgery over, she tidied up, received a few instructions about the evening surgery, refused his offer of coffee and went down the street to the shop. Mrs Simpkins sold everything, or such was her proud boast and sure enough from the depths of her shop she produced a small plastic pot.

'That's what I call sensible,' she declared. 'Miss Brimble never thought of it. Well, a maiden lady such as she were wouldn't 'ave, would she? A real blessing it'll be for all the mums with little 'uns.'

She peered across the counter through the shop window. 'Doctor's just gone past so you can pop across with it.'

Which Matilda did.

At home she found her mother in the best of good spirits. Mrs Milton would be going to Taunton on Wednesday and had offered her a lift. 'You only work in the morning,' she reminded Matilda, 'so you can be here with your father. I don't know how long I shall be gone; perhaps Mrs Milton will ask me to tea. Will you make some coffee? Your father has a headache; a cup might make him feel better. I must iron a few things—perhaps you would get a fire going in the sitting room? It's such a miserable day.'

After lunch Matilda, in an old mac and headscarf, went into the garden. The back garden was quite large and so overgrown it was hard to see what it was once like. But almost hidden against the end fence were the chrysanthemums, deep pink and a bit bedraggled. She picked the best of them, filled a vase for the living room and put the rest in a plastic bag to take with her to the surgery that evening. And while she was about it she rooted round in the garden shed and found two vases. No longer neglected, the chrysanthemums perked up, in one vase on the waiting-room table, and the other on the windowsill in the surgery. Several patients remarked upon them but if the doctor noticed he didn't choose to say anything…

In fact, he had seen them the moment he entered the surgery, given them a quick glance and turned his attention to his first patient. He hoped that Matilda wasn't going to strew cushions around the place or nur-

ture pot plants on the windowsills. Perhaps he had better nip any such ideas in the bud...

But he had no chance to do so that evening; a farm
worker on one of the outlying farms had fallen off a
ladder and he was needed there. He left with a brisk
goodnight, leaving Matilda to pack up and lock the
doors. And, of course, the next day there was no surgery until the evening.

When she got there he was already at his desk, writing, and she made haste to get out the patients' notes,
and when the phone rang, which it did continuously,
answered it. It wasn't until she ushered out the last
patient that Dr Lovell came into the waiting room.

Matilda was on her knees, grovelling under the row
of chairs collecting the toys the smaller patients had
been playing with, so she was not at her best.

His cool, 'Miss Paige,' brought her to her feet,
pleased to see him but unhappily aware that she wasn't
looking her best.

'I see that you have introduced one or two—er—
innovations. And while I appreciate your efforts I must
beg you not to make too many drastic alterations.'

Matilda tucked a wisp of hair behind an ear. 'Well,
I won't,' she assured him. 'Only the umbrellas dripping
all over the floor are nasty and you can't expect a toddler to perch on a loo, you know. And I thought a few
flowers would cheer the place up a bit. A potted plant
or two?' she added hopefully.

'If you have set your heart on that, by all means, but
I must make it clear that I do not wish for a plant in
my surgery.'

She said warmly, 'Oh, do they give you hay fever
or something?'

The doctor, self-assured and used to being treated

with a certain amount of respect, found himself at a loss for a reply. Being in the habit of advising others as to their various illnesses, he hardly expected to hear an opinion passed as to his own health.

When Matilda got back from the Wednesday morning clinic her mother had already left with Mrs Milton.

'Most fortunate,' her father observed as they drank their coffee together, 'that your mother has the opportunity to enjoy a day out; she has so few pleasures.'

'Well,' said Matilda, 'Mrs Milton is going to introduce Mother to her friends and I'm sure she will be asked to join in the social life around here. I suppose there is some…'

'Oh, I believe so. Lady Truscott has a large circle of friends; your mother will enjoy meeting them.' He added, 'Perhaps there will be some young people for you, my dear.'

She agreed cheerfully. She would have dearly liked to go dancing, play tennis, and even venture into amateur theatricals, but only if the doctor was there too, and somehow she couldn't imagine him as an actor. Tennis, yes—he would be a good tennis player and a good dancer—a bit on the conservative side, perhaps. She allowed herself a few moments of daydreaming, waltzing around some magnificent ballroom in his arms. She would, of course, be exquisitely dressed and so very pretty that she was the object of all eyes… But only Dr Lovell's eyes mattered.

Not that he showed any signs of interest in her at the surgery; indeed, she had the strong feeling that as a person she just wasn't there—a pair of hands, yes, and a voice for the telephone and someone to find old notes. He was engaged to be married, she reminded herself, and quite rightly didn't notice any female other than his betrothed…

Later in the day Mrs Paige came back from Taunton, bubbling over with the delights of her day.

'A marvellous hairdresser, Matilda, worth every penny, and the shops are excellent. Of course I had no money but next time there are several things I simply must have.' She gave a little laugh. 'I'm to go with Mrs Milton to Lady Truscott's—the next committee meeting for some charity or other—so I must smarten up a little. You wouldn't want your mother to look shabby, would you?'

Her father said, 'My dear, I'm sure I can let you have a little extra. Matilda should have her own money to spend how she likes.'

Matilda slipped out of the room. She had heard her father's mild remonstrance often enough but it went unheeded. Once the outstanding bills had been paid she would go to Taunton herself and buy some new clothes, have her hair done, a manicure, new cosmetics… Dr Lovell hadn't noticed her yet; perhaps he never would. He was going to marry, she reminded herself then, and remembered that Mrs Simpkins hadn't liked his fiancée.

Matilda, peeling potatoes, made up her mind to find out more about her.

After morning surgery next day, since it was a fine day with a strong wind blowing, she filled the washing machine and went into the garden and began to sweep up the leaves lying thick on the neglected grass, suitably but unglamorously dressed in an elderly sweater and skirt and wellies. Since there was no one to see, she had tied her hair back with a bit of string from the garden shed. She had found a rake there and set to with a will, for the moment happy; her small worries were forgotten as she planned just how the garden would look once she had tamed its wildness and cared for it. She paused to lean on the rake.

'Roses,' she decided, 'and lavender and peonies and lupins and hollyhocks.'

She had been talking to herself, something she quite often did even if Rastus wasn't there to listen. 'It'll look lovely, I promise you.'

She flung an arm wide and nearly fell over when the doctor said, an inch or so from her ear. 'Do you often talk to yourself?'

She shot round to face him and he thought that she looked quite pretty with colour in her cheeks and her hair hanging loose.

'Of course not.' She sounded tart. 'I was talking to the garden. Flowers like being talked to. The Prince of Wales talks to his…'

'So he does.' The doctor sounded mild. 'I've never found the time.'

'No—well, of course I don't suppose you would. Anyway, you would want to spend it with your…'

She paused, not liking the cold look he gave her. She went on quickly. 'Is it me you want to see about something? Or father…?'

'Your father.' He watched her idly. The shabby clothes she was wearing did nothing for her but he had to admit that he liked her hair—and he was intrigued by her naturalness. Not his type, of course…

He said briskly, 'Your father is home?'

'Oh, yes. He'll be in his study—he's writing a book.'

She led the way to the front door, kicked off her wellies and ushered him into the narrow hall. 'Mother's in the sitting room…'

'I'll see your father first if I may.'

Matilda put her head round the study door. 'Father, here's Dr Lovell to see you.'

He went past her with a brief nod and closed the door gently behind him, and as he did so her mother came out of the sitting room. 'Who is that?' She frowned. 'You should have fetched me, Matilda...'

'Dr Lovell said he'd see father first.'

'Well, you go back into the garden; I'll have a talk with him.'

Mrs Paige went back to the sitting room and had a look in the old-fashioned mirror over the fireplace. She looked all right, she decided, but it wouldn't harm her to add a little lipstick. And perhaps a touch more powder...

Dr Lovell shook hands with his patient and drew up a chair. He said easily, 'I've had all your notes from your previous doctor—Dr Grant, wasn't it? I've met him; you couldn't have been in better hands. But I'd like you to tell me how you feel now and then perhaps I might take a look at you?'

He took his time, listening patiently to Mr Paige's vague recital of how he felt. 'Of course, I'm aware that I may have another heart attack at any time, but I feel well; I find it most restful living here and I have my writing, and possibly later on I shall be able to assist Mr Milton from time to time should he wish it.'

Dr Lovell listened gravely and said presently, 'Well, if I might take a look?'

That done, he sat back in his chair. 'As far as I can judge you are in excellent shape. I shall write you up for some different pills and I advise you to take a walk each day. Well wrapped up and for half an hour.

Taking reasonable precautions you should be able to enjoy a normal life.'

'Splendid. I feel a fraud that you should visit me; I could quite well come to your surgery.'

'Better that I look in on you from time to time, but let me know if you are worried about anything.'

'Indeed I will; Matilda can always take a message. I hope she is proving satisfactory? She seems very happy working at your surgery. Perhaps she will meet some young people once she gets to know the village. She leads a quiet life and, of course, she is indispensable to my wife here in the house.' Mr Paige nodded contentedly. 'We are indeed lucky to have such a caring daughter.'

The doctor, who almost never thought of Matilda, felt a sudden pang of pity for her, destined to play the role of dutiful daughter—and why was she indispensable to her mother?

'Your wife is an invalid?'

'No, no, nothing like that, but she has always been delicate—her nerves.'

So the doctor was forewarned when he found Mrs Paige waiting for him in the sitting-room doorway.

She held out a hand. 'Dr Lovell, so good of you to come. I do worry so much about my husband; it upsets me so. My wretched nerves…' She smiled up at him. 'I'm not at all strong and having to move here to this poky little house has upset me, too. My husband loves it and so does Matilda, so I suppose I must learn to make a new life. They are both content with so little.'

He said blandly, 'I'm sure you will be glad to know that Mr Paige is doing well. I've advised him to go out for a short time each day for a brisk walk.'

'Such a pity we gave up the car. But, of course, he

doesn't drive any more and I have never learned. ' She gave a little laugh. 'Silly me.'

'Your daughter drives?'

'Matilda? Oh, yes, but there was no point in keeping the car just for her. Won't you come and sit down for a while?'

'I'm afraid I can't stay; I'm on my afternoon round.' He smiled—a professional smile with no warmth—and shook hands and went out of the open door into the garden.

Matilda was still raking leaves but when she saw him she went to meet him. 'Father? He's all right? I won't keep you; you are on your visits, aren't you?'

She went with him to his car and he said, 'He's pretty fit. I'll give you some pills for him and please see that he walks for a while each day. Let me know if you are worried.' His smile was kind.

He got in and drove away with a casual nod and she watched the grey Bentley slide away down the lane. She thought about the smile; he had looked quite different for a moment. She wondered what he was really like beneath his calm, professional face. Would she ever find out? He was courteous towards her but in a cool, offhand way which daunted her; quite obviously he had no wish to add warmth to their relationship.

And quite right too, reflected Matilda that evening, nodding her sensible head. If I were engaged to marry someone I wouldn't bother with anyone else. She wished very much that she could meet his fiancée, for, loving him as she did, it was important to her that he should be happy.

'I am a fool,' said Matilda, addressing Rastus, making the pastry for a steak and kidney pie. The butcher's van called twice a week in the village and it was a meal that her father enjoyed. Rastus gave her a long, considering look and turned his back.

There was always pay day to cheer her up. She prudently paid most of her wages into the bank and crossed the street to the shop, intent on buying one or two extras for the larder. She also needed tights and toothpaste, and Mrs Simpkins stocked a certain shampoo guaranteed to bring out the highlights on one's hair.

The shop was quite full. Matilda wasn't the only one to be paid on a Friday, and Mrs Simpkins was doing a brisk trade, enjoying a good gossip at the same time. Matilda, waiting her turn, listened to the odd snippets of gossip. Bill Gates up at Hill Farm had had to have the vet out to one of his cows. Triplets, doing well. Time he had a bit of luck. There had been a small fire out at Pike's place—a chip pan left on the stove. 'And what do you expect from that Maisie Coffin? She bain't no housewife...' There were matronly nods all round in agreement and Matilda felt a pang of sympathy for Maisie.

'Coming this weekend, so I hear?' said a stout matron, waiting for her bacon to be sliced. 'Staying with Dr Lovell, of course, bringing that brother of hers with her.'

Matilda edged a little nearer, anxious not to miss anything.

'Time they married,' said another voice. 'Though she is not to my liking, mind you. A real town lady; don't want nothing to do with the likes of us.'

There was a murmur of agreement. 'But pretty as a picture,' said another voice.

Mrs Simpkins spoke up. 'Men don't want a pretty

picture for a wife; they wants a wife to make an 'ome for 'im and kiddies. And 'im such a good man, too.'

There was a collective sigh of regret and Matilda wondered what the doctor would say if he could hear the gossip about him. She didn't think that he would mind; he would be amused. And he had no need to worry; he was well liked and respected. In the eyes of the village he was on a par with the Reverend Mr Milton.

Matilda bought her tights and toothpaste and a hand cream Mrs Simpkins assured her was just the thing if she was going to do a lot of gardening. She added back bacon, a cauliflower, cooking apples and a packet of chocolate biscuits to her purchases, answered Mrs Simpkins' questions as to life at the surgery and how her mother and father were.

'If the weather's all right, I hope Father will be able to come to church on Sunday,' said Matilda. 'And, of course, Mother will be with him. Mr Milton has kindly offered to drive them to church.'

'You too?'

'Well, yes, I hope so...'

Mrs Simpkins nodded. 'Time you got around a bit and met a few of us. Church is as good a place as any.'

Matilda said that, yes, she was quite right, and went off home. It was a dry day and she would be able to get into the garden. Her mother, with the prospect of going to church on Sunday, was happy. She would meet some of the people Mrs Milton had mentioned and it was a splendid opportunity for people in the village to get to know them. She fell to wondering what she should wear until Mr Paige said gently, 'My dear, we are going to church, not a social gathering.' He smiled lovingly at her and turned to Matilda. 'My dear, a man is coming to re-connect the telephone on Monday; your mother—we both feel it is a necessity.'

'Yes, Father. Did you have a letter about it?'

'Yes, it's on my desk, I believe. I should have thought that it could have been done without cost for there has been a telephone here previously, but it seems there is a payment to make.'

Matilda, finding it buried under a pile of books, saw that if she had had any ideas about spending next week's wages on anything she could forget them. And, to be on the safe side, she warned her mother that that particular bill would have to be paid at once. News which Mrs Paige took with some annoyance. 'I was hoping that you could lend me some money; I simply must have a few things. I'll pay you back when your father gets his pension.'

'I'm sorry, Mother; once the bills are paid...'

'Bills, bills, why can't they wait? Really, Matilda, you're nothing but a prig—too good to be true. I suppose you tell everyone that you hand over your money each week because it's your saintly duty to do so.'

Matilda said quietly, 'No, I don't tell anyone, Mother.' She sighed. 'I expect you're right. I'm not quite sure what a prig is exactly, but it sounds like me. I've been a disappointment to myself. I should have liked to have been pretty and clever and well dressed, I should have liked the chance to go dancing and have fun, but there was always some reason why I didn't— helping Father in the parish, taking over most of the household chores so that you had more time to be the vicar's wife and any chance I might have had to leave home and get a job is finally squashed, isn't it?'

She saw from her mother's face that she wasn't really listening. She said woodenly, 'I'm going into the garden.'

Digging the flowerbeds, cutting back overgrown shrubs, grubbing up weeds helped, and all the while she cried, tears rolling down her cheeks while she sniffed and grizzled. But she felt better presently and when she went indoors she looked very much as usual.

On Saturday morning she walked down to the village armed with the grocery list. It was a long one and she saw that she would have to supplement the housekeeping with some of her own money.

'Let me know how much you spent,' her mother had said. 'I'll let you have it back when your father gives me the month's housekeeping.'

Matilda was walking back, with two plastic shopping bags weighing her down, and had reached the doctor's house when its handsome door was opened and three people emerged—the doctor, a short, thick-set man, a good deal younger than he, and a young woman. A very handsome one, too, Matilda saw out of the corner of her eye. She was tall and fair and slim and dressed in the height of fashion. Not quite suitable for Much Winterlow, reflected Matilda, allowing herself to be catty, but the woman was distinctly eye-catching.

They came down the short path to the gate set in the iron railings separating the house from the street, and had reached it as Matilda drew level with it. The doctor wished her good morning. 'Been shopping?' he asked.

Well, of course; any idiot could see that, thought Matilda. But he was being polite. She said 'Yes,' and 'Good morning, Doctor,' and walked on.

She wasn't out of earshot when she heard the young woman's voice—well modulated but carrying. 'What a quaint little thing,' she remarked.

And what had she meant by that? reflected Matilda.
She had reached the field and could utter her thoughts
out loud. 'I'm plain and a bit dowdy, I suppose, but
otherwise I look as normal as anyone else. Well, I
shan't let it upset me.'

All the same she dressed carefully for church on
Sunday—her good suit of timeless cut, and the small
felt hat which went with it. Her gloves and shoes had
seen better days but they were good and she didn't
need a handbag; she tucked her collection money into
her glove.

Mrs Milton came early to fetch them and since
Matilda was not quite ready, her mother and father
were driven away in the car and she walked to the
village, getting to the church just as the bell ceased.

The congregation was quite large and she saw that
her mother and father were sitting in one of the front
pews with Mrs Milton, but her plan to slip into a pew
at the back of the church was frustrated by her mother
who had turned round and seen her. When she reached
the pew she saw the doctor and his guests sitting on
the opposite side of the aisle just behind them. She had
only a glimpse as she went past but it was enough to
see that the girl with him was the picture of elegance…

Matilda reminded herself that she was in church as
she said her prayers and sang the hymns and listened
to the sermon, but once the service was over and they
were outside in the churchyard, meeting various people
kind Mrs Milton was introducing to her mother and
father, she allowed her thoughts to dwell on the doctor
and his companions, standing close by, talking to Lady
Truscott. She edged away from them and took shelter
behind Mrs Milton, only to find the two groups
merging.

Mrs Milton said, 'Of course you've met Mr and Mrs Paige, haven't you? And Matilda works for you.'

She looked enquiringly at him and he said easily, 'Two friends of mine, spending the weekend: Lucilla Armstrong and her brother Guy.'

He turned to look at them. 'Mrs Milton, the vicar's wife, and the Reverend Mr Paige and Mrs Paige—and their daughter Matilda.'

Lucilla acknowledged the introductions with a cool nod. 'We saw you yesterday.' Her eyes roamed over Matilda's person. 'I wondered who you were.'

Matilda said in a matter-of-fact voice, 'I'd been to do the shopping. I'm surprised that you remembered me. I must have looked quaint laden down with plastic bags.' She smiled sweetly and the doctor choked back a laugh. Miss Matilda Paige had revealed an unexpected side of her nature—or was he mistaken? Had her remark been as guileless as her ordinary face?

There was polite talk for a few more minutes before Mrs Milton said, 'We mustn't stand around too long. I'm going to drive Mr and Mrs Paige back home—and you too, of course, Matilda.' She smiled at the circle of faces around her.

'I hope you have a pleasant weekend here. I'm sure it's good for Henry to relax from his work.'

Henry, thought Matilda, taking care not to look at him. A nice old-fashioned English name. She looked at his other guest instead. Guy Armstrong was good-looking, she conceded, but he had a weak chin and he laughed too much; besides, by the time he was forty he would be fat...

She added her polite goodbyes to everyone else's and got into Mrs Milton's car, sitting in the back with her father because her mother wanted to ask about some extra committee Mrs Milton had suggested that she might like to join.

And back home over lunch, while her mother talked animatedly of the people she had met at church and the prospect of a social life even if limited to the village, Matilda had ample free time to think about Dr Lovell. She thought about Lucilla, too, who would be an ideal wife for him. She was not as young as Matilda had first thought—indeed, Lucilla must be edging very close to thirty—but she was so beautifully cared for that no man would believe that... And, of course, her lovely clothes helped.

I'm jealous, thought Matilda, but I can't help that. I should be glad that he has found someone who will make him happy.

She went to the kitchen to wash up, while her mother, still happily making plans, went with her father to the sitting room.

'Perhaps I should find another job.' Matilda addressed Rastus, who gave her a considering look before tucking into his dinner. 'But if I did I'd not see him, would I? And I couldn't bear that. Of course when they marry she will get me the sack. She doesn't like me, which is silly, for I'm hardly a rival, am I?'

Rastus, nicely full, sat and stared at her. 'You're not much help, are you?'' said Matilda.

It was pouring with rain on Monday morning. Matilda, wringing herself dry before she opened the surgery door, mopped her face and tugged her wet hair back into a semblance of tidiness and, still a bit damp, got out the notes for the morning's patients. She then opened the door, casting a quick look round the waiting room as she did so. It was spotlessly clean and the chrysanthemums she had brought from the garden made a cheerful spot of colour beside the tidy pile of magazines on the table; the place was nicely warm too.

The first patients arrived, shedding wet macs, umbrellas and leaving muddy marks on the floor, and punctually at eight o'clock the doctor opened his door and requested the first patient.

By the time the last patient had left it was well past ten o'clock. Matilda started to tidy the place, lock away the notes, rearrange the magazines and collect up forgotten gloves, a scarf or two and a child's plastic toy, and, tucked away in a corner, a shopping bag of groceries. She would take it over to Mrs Simpkins' shop since the surgery door would be locked...

The door opened and the doctor stood looking at her.

'You had better have a cup of coffee before you go,' he said briskly.

Matilda put the shopping bag on the table. 'Thank you, Doctor, but I'd rather not stop.'

'You mustn't allow hurt pride to interfere with common sense,' he observed. 'Far be it from me to send you out into this weather without so much as a warm drink inside you.'

'Hurt pride?' said Matilda, and then added, 'Oh, the first morning when you told me not to watch the clock. Oh, that's all right; I'm not one to bear a grudge!'

She smiled and went past him into the surgery where the coffee tray stood on his desk.

'You are happy working here?' asked Dr Lovell, taking his coffee and offering her a biscuit from the tin.

'Yes, thank you.'

'It is rather a quiet life for you,' went on the doctor. 'Miss Armstrong wondered if you found life here dull.'

'How kind of her to concern herself about me,' said Matilda in a quiet voice which gave away none of the powerful rage engulfing her. The interfering busybody... A first step towards getting her the sack.

'She pointed out that you are very young for such a dull job. Of course Miss Brimble was elderly.'

'As long as you are satisfied with my work,' said Matilda, 'I wish to stay here. And if I stay long enough I'll be elderly like Miss Brimble! Won't I?'

She put down her coffee cup. 'Is there anything you would like me to do before I go?'

'No, I think not.'

'Thank you for the coffee. I'll be here this evening.'

She skipped through the door, locked up and went out into the rain, crossing the road to the shop.

'Someone left their groceries at the surgery,' she told Mrs Simpkins. 'Shall I leave the bag here? Or if you know who the owner is I could take it.'

'Bless you, miss; that's a kind thought. It's old Mrs Harding's weekly shopping. Lives just down the street, number fourteen on the other side. She's that forgetful. If it's not troubling you...'

Mrs Simpkins leaned comfortably across the counter. 'Saw you in church,' she said. 'Very nice you looked, too—a sight better than that madam with our doctor. Mrs Inch—'is 'ousekeeper, you know—told me she acted like she was in an 'otel. Can't think what 'e sees in 'er.'

'She's quite beautiful,' said Matilda. 'I'll have a piece of tasty cheese, Mrs Simpkins, and some of those dry cheese biscuits.'

Mrs Simpkins reached for the cheese. 'Bin inside 'is 'ouse? Lovely, so I'm told—furniture 'anded down from way back in the family. Bin in the village for

years and years. 'E don't need to earn 'is living, of
course; plenty of family money as you might say. A
fine catch for that Miss Armstrong.'

She reached up for a packet of biscuits. 'I hear your
mum's going to Lady Truscott's for the charity committee meeting. Don't see much of 'er in the village,
though. Poorly, is she, like your dad?'

'No, no, Mother's very well, but you know how it
is when you move house. But we've settled in nicely
and my father is so much better now that he has retired.'

Matilda said goodbye, and left to deliver the shopping bag, then hurry home in the rain. Mrs Simpkins,
watching her go, thought what a dull life she must lead
with two elderly parents and no young man.

Another week went by and another pay day, and
even after bolstering up the housekeeping purse and
paying the small outstanding debts Matilda had some
money. True, her mother had wheedled some of it for
herself so that she might go to Taunton once again.
She must look her best when she went to Lady
Truscott's, she'd pointed out; she would make do with
the clothes she had but her hair must be trimmed and
set and a few highlights added. Surely Matilda could
understand that. 'And really you have nothing to spend
your money on, Matilda. There's nothing to be done
about your hair except bundle it up like you do, and
you don't need to look fashionable. No one sees you
at the surgery and you've got that winter coat once it
gets really cold.'

All of which was perfectly true. Matilda said nothing
for the simple reason that if she did she might say
something she would regret afterwards.

But on the following Tuesday, her day free until eve-

ning surgery, she took the local bus to Taunton. She
hadn't told her mother or father that she was going
until she'd taken them their early morning tea.

'That's right my dear,' said her father. 'You go and
have a pleasant day. Have you sufficient money?'

She kissed the top of his head. 'Yes, thank you,
Father.'

There was no chance to say more for her mother had
sat bolt upright in bed. 'You're going to Taunton? Why
didn't you tell me? I could have gone with you; I need
several things. How thoughtless of you, Matilda—and
why do you want to go?'

'To shop,' said Matilda, 'and I must go now or I'll
miss the bus. I'll be back before tea.'

'I should feel mean, but I don't,' said Matilda to
herself, hurrying down to the bus stop outside Mrs
Simpkins'. There were several people there already,
and the doctor, standing at his dining-room window,
watched her join the little group. He thought idly that
if he had known she had wanted to go to Taunton he
would have given her a lift for he would be at the
hospital for most of the day. He turned away and went
to eat his breakfast.

Matilda hadn't much money but she knew what she
wanted. The doctor only saw her during surgery hours,
so it made sense to make herself as attractive as possible during that time. Well, not sense, actually, since
he never looked at her, but even if she had no hope
that he would like her that wasn't going to stop her
from doing something about her looks.

Silly, really, thought Matilda, making for the shops.
It would have to be Marks & Spencer; she hadn't

enough money for any of the smart boutiques. She would go there first, anyway...

Maybe the doctor would never look at her; she would still find solace in the wearing of the grey jersey dress she found almost at once. It was suitably short but not too much so and it had a white collar and pretty buttons, and since it was jersey it wouldn't crease.

And there was some money left over—enough for a navy sweater to wear with her last year's pleated skirt. She checked the money in her purse then, had a cup of coffee and a roll, and went in search of something tasty for supper, as well as the boiled sweets her father liked to suck while he worked and a tiny bottle of the perfume her mother liked.

By then it was time to get the bus back to Much Winterlow.

CHAPTER THREE

THE bus went from the castle buildings and Matilda had overlooked the fact that she had walked some distance from it. She hurried now; there was no other bus; it was a once-weekly event. Much Winterlow was far too isolated to merit more than that and how would she get back if she missed it? She broke into a run, much hampered by her parcels.

Dr Lovell, driving himself home after a day at Trinity Hospital, caught sight of her as he turned the car into East Street from North Street. She was dancing with impatience, waiting for the lights to allow her to cross over to the bus depot, now tantalisingly close. He turned the car into the bus park and stopped by the bus. He opened his door and got out as she came galloping along.

'Cut it rather fine, haven't you?' he asked, took her parcels from her and popped her into the car.

Matilda, too breathless to speak, sat wordless as he drove back into the traffic and took the road home. Presently she said, 'Thank you, Doctor,' and then added, 'I've been shopping...'

'One tends to forget the time,' he observed, and then he said nothing more. So she looked out of the window at the gathering dusk and wished that she could think of something interesting or witty to say.

They were nearly at the village when he spoke again. 'Surgery starts in just over an hour. I suggest that

46

you have your tea at my place. You're on the phone?
I'll ring your mother when we get there.'

He added, 'And don't argue; it's the sensible thing
to do.'

It was hardly an invitation, more like a command,
but it was good sense, too. She would have no time to
spare if she went home. She thanked him in a stiff
manner and followed him into the house after he'd
drawn up at his front door.

The interior, she saw at a glance, bore out the charm
of the exterior. The hall was square with panelled walls
and a staircase with barley-sugar balusters rising from
its centre to the gallery above. There was a long case
clock and facing it a pair of cane-backed chairs flank-
ing a side table upon which was a Staffordshire china
bowl filled with autumn flowers.

She would have liked to stand and stare but the doctor was urging her across the hall and Mrs Inch had
come through the baize door at the back of the hall.

'Ah, Mrs Inch, if we might have tea? It is too late
for Miss Paige to go home before surgery.'

'Give me a few minutes, Doctor, and I dare say Miss
Paige would like to tidy herself.'

Her long, rather solemn face gave the hint of a smile
and she whisked Matilda down the hall and into a
charming cloakroom, equipped with everything anyone
could possibly want and two mirrors, one full-length,
the other over the handbasin. Matilda took a quick look
at her reflection and sighed, combed her hair and
washed her hands and went back into the hall.

The doctor, waiting for her, flung open a door. 'In
here, Miss Paige.'

Very polite, thought Matilda, but not much warmth,
and she walked into the room.

It was light and airy by reason of the bay window overlooking the garden at the back of the house. There was an open door beside the window and she could see green lawns and flowerbeds, still colourful with autumn flowers and the last roses. And there was a dog racing around, a large, woolly-coated animal with a feathery tail.

'Oh, you've got a dog...?'

She went to the door and the doctor followed her.

'Yes. Sam. You like dogs?'

'Yes. Once we're settled I'd like to have one.'

'They're good company. Come and have your tea.'

She sat down near the log fire burning in the wide fireplace. Mrs Inch had put the tea tray on a low table and as he sat down in a winged armchair opposite her the doctor said, 'I gave your mother a quick call to let her know you're here. Will you pour out?'

When she had passed him his cup and saucer he said, 'You have had a pleasant time in Taunton?'

'Yes, thank you.' She had been brought up to make conversation and put the numerous visitors to her father's house at their ease; so she embarked on a pleasant conversation now and the doctor, amused, encouraged her.

While she talked she looked around her discreetly. It was a splendid room, she decided. There was a William and Mary tapestry settee which could have graced a museum, tripod tables with piecrust edges, a side table with marquetry decorations and a carved court cupboard. There were flowers and several comfortable chairs which blended in nicely with the antiques. The walls were covered in a cream striped wallpaper and hung with paintings, and there were silver wall-sconces. A lovely room but warm and lived in.

When offered a second of Mrs Inch's delicious scones, Matilda accepted it. She was hungry and her lunch had been a meagre affair.

The doctor, watching her eating a slice of sponge cake and, when pressed, a piece of shortbread, was surprised to feel a pang of concern. She was enjoying her tea with the pleasure of a hungry child offered an unexpected treat. And he had seen her glances around the room. He had long ago taken it for granted, but she, discovering its beauty for the first time, positively glowed with delight.

It was almost time for surgery; Matilda bent to stroke Sam's woolly head and got up. The doctor got up, too, and listened gravely to her thanks. He was quite disarmed by her. 'I was hungry and it was a lovely tea, and I'm very grateful for the lift back.'

He said kindly, 'It was a pleasure to have company, Miss Paige.' He opened the door, crossed the hall with her and opened the door leading to the surgery.

There weren't many patients and he left to go to one of the outlying farms the moment the last patient had gone, leaving her to lock up and then go home. When she got there, with supper to get, she found her mother was lying down with a headache.

'Now you're back I think I shall stay in bed and have something light on a tray.' Mrs Paige added sharply, 'You should have come straight home instead of having tea at Dr Lovell's house. I suppose he felt he had to ask you out of politeness.'

Matilda said merely, 'It was a nice tea; besides, there wasn't much time before the evening surgery.'

'Well, what do you expect if you go off for the day?' Mrs Paige eyed Matilda's shopping bags. 'You spent all your money, I suppose.'

'Yes, Mother.' There was no point in showing her mother what she had bought; it would be the wrong colour, or in poor taste or unfashionable... No one was likely to notice and by no one Matilda meant Dr Lovell. But she reminded herself she would enjoy wearing them.

Whilst getting the supper, she pictured him, back home by now—she hoped—sitting by the fire with Sam at his feet, waiting for Mrs Inch to give him his supper. And, that over, he would return to the comfort of his fireside and read or watch the TV. She hoped he wouldn't sit up too late; he had had a busy day...

He was, in fact, delivering premature twins in an isolated cottage and then driving to Taunton behind the ambulance he had called. He stayed to make sure that the mother and babies were in good shape and then took the father back home before going to his own bed in the small hours.

Matilda heard of this when she arrived at the surgery in the morning—not that the doctor had mentioned it to anyone, but a neighbour had told another neighbour and they had told the boy who brought the milk down to the village. The surgery finished, Matilda wondered if she should mention the news to the doctor and decided against it; he looked as well turned out as usual, his manner as calm as always, but she could see that he was tired.

Only after the evening surgery—a particularly heavy one—as she bade him goodnight, did she say in her sensible way, 'I hope you will be able to get a good night's sleep, Doctor. You must be tired.'

He gave her a look from cold eyes. 'Thank you, Miss

Paige, but you have no need to concern yourself about me.'

'Oh, I'm not concerned about you; I'm sure you're well able to look after yourself,' said Matilda kindly. She went on chattily, 'Of course, being a clergyman's daughter, I'm in the habit of concerning myself about people. Some people call it being a Nosy Parker.'

She made for the door. 'Goodnight, Doctor. You'll feel more yourself after a good night's sleep.'

The doctor stared at the closed door for a few moments. Then he laughed. There had been something different about Matilda although he had no idea what it might be.

Matilda, hanging the grey dress in the wardrobe ready for the morning, would have been pleased to know that; he might not have noticed the new dress but at least he had been aware that there was something unusual...

Her mother hadn't thought much of it. 'Though I suppose it's suitable for your work. I mean, no one would notice it, would they?' She had added crossly, 'I hope you don't intend to spend all your money on clothes for yourself, Matilda?'

Which was such an unfair remark that Matilda hadn't answered it.

It was fortunate that Mrs Paige was beginning to be invited out to coffee or tea by the various ladies of Mrs Milton's acquaintance, so beyond complaining that she had nothing fit to wear she began to find that life in a small village wasn't so bad after all. She left the shopping to Matilda, of course, and a good deal of the housework. As she pointed out, Mr Paige was now so much better, he could be left for a few hours. After all, he spent so much time in his study, he was seldom aware of anyone else being in the house.

Matilda was uneasy about this, for frequently she left home to go to the surgery in the late afternoon and her mother had not returned. But her father was happy, working away at his book, taking the short walks Dr Lovell had suggested, and glad to see that his wife was becoming content with their new way of life. He was happily oblivious of the mundane problems which Matilda dealt with.

She had no reason to be dissatisfied with life, reflected Matilda. They were managing nicely now; there was even enough money over for her mother to have her trips to Taunton, although Matilda could see that they might have to be curtailed once the winter set in properly and the gas and coal bills mounted...

She enjoyed her job; by now she knew everyone in the village, and although she doubted if the doctor had anything other than a detached acceptance of her presence at least they were on speaking terms.

And that was all she could ever expect of him, she supposed.

She was wrong.

It was a casual traveller, having lost his way and stopping to enquire at Mrs Simpkins' shop, who brought the flu to Much Winterlow. The shop was full at the time, since it was Friday afternoon and housewives, armed with a weekly pay packet, were intent on stocking up for the weekend. The man lingered while several voices told him which road to take, and since he was coughing a good deal Mrs Simpkins sold him some lozenges and several ladies offered advice as to the best way to treat a bad cold such as he had...

It was the following week when the first victims

came to the surgery. Matilda, viewing the steadily increasing ranks of miserable, coughing patients, decided to keep the surgery doors open for a little longer each day. She didn't think the doctor would notice; in any case he would never go away before he had seen the last patient.

But he did notice, of course. After a morning surgery which had overshot its length by half an hour he observed that since the surgery seemed to have lengthened its hours it might be as well if the morning surgery was kept open for half an hour longer. 'And an hour longer in the evening. If this flu gets worse, we shall have to tackle it as best we can. We can't expect much outside help; the hospitals in Taunton and Yeovil are already full. Ideally patients should stay at home and be nursed there. I've asked for nursing help but there is a shortage there too.'

'I've got my first aid certificate,' said Matilda. 'I'll help.'

He looked up from his desk. 'An offer which I accept but which I hope you won't come to regret, Miss Paige.'

Towards the end of the week it became obvious that the flu was getting a firm grip on the village. It was difficult to keep it in check, for people still had to go about their business, shopping had to be done, and workers taking the bus to the small furniture factory some miles away coughed and sneezed and spread their germs. That they would have preferred to stay at home in bed was a foregone conclusion, but most of them were on piece work and needed the money.

Matilda, explaining to her mother and father, met with instant opposition from Mrs Paige.

'You mean to say you offered to work longer hours?
You're bound to catch this flu, and what if you give it
to us? How very selfish of you, Matilda.'

Her father said, 'You do what you think is right, my
dear. Your mother and I will be perfectly all right…'

Matilda gave him a grateful smile. 'Well, I thought
it might be a good idea if I got a room in the village,
just while this epidemic lasts. I'll be working longer
hours and going to and fro might get difficult. I'll come
home whenever I can and bring whatever you need,
but I won't see you. Luckily you're on the outskirts of
the village.'

'Where will you get a room? And who is to pay for
it?' asked her mother.

'Mrs Simpkins knows several people who let rooms
in the summer. And I'm to be paid for the extra hours.'

'I should hope so. When will you go?'

'I'll see Mrs Simpkins in the morning and ask her
to help.'

The morning surgery was packed and afterwards Dr
Lovell went away at once to visit his more seriously
ill patients in their homes. Matilda tidied up, drank the
coffee Mrs Inch brought her, locked up and went across
the street to the shop.

There were several customers, buying what they
needed briskly, not stopping for the comfortable gossip
which was their habit, and when the shop was empty
Matilda asked, 'I wonder if you would help me, Mrs
Simpkins?'

Mrs Simpkins, deprived of her cosy chats, was all
eagerness.

'Course I will, love. What d'yer want?'

'A room,' said Matilda, 'and meals, just till this flu

is over. I'm working longer hours and I need to be near the surgery and I don't want to give the flu to my mother and father.'

'Quite right, my dear. And I know just the person—Mrs Trickett, three doors down. She's 'ad it, so she won't be afraid of you giving it to her. She'll be glad of the money. You go along and see her; say I sent you.' She eyed Matilda. ''Aving to work 'ard, I'll be bound. And the doctor out all hours. Can't get 'elp, I'm told. 'Ospitals all full to bursting. 'E 'ad to drive old Mrs Crouch to Bridgewater to get 'er into a bed. Pneumonia and very poorly. You're not scared at getting it?'

Matilda said that, no, she wasn't. Indeed she hadn't thought much about it; all she could really think about was seeing more of Dr Lovell and being able to help him.

Mrs Trickett lived in a very small thatched cottage. Its front door opened onto the street and inside it was crammed with furniture and an enormous number of china ornaments and knick-knacks. But the little bedroom she was shown was spotlessly clean. There was no bathroom. She could go across to the Lovell Arms, said Mrs Trickett, and have a bath there.

'There's a lovely bathroom. There's a jug and basin in the room for a wash and I'll give you your meals.' She looked uncertain. 'It's not much...'

'It's fine,' said Matilda. 'Just what I want. I can nip to and from the surgery. I have to be there well before eight o'clock in the morning and perhaps I may get held up and not get back on time. Would you mind?'

'Lor' bess you, miss, no. You'll come?'

'Please. Shall I pay you each week? I don't suppose

it will be for long, and I'll pay in advance. And I'll go and see the landlord at the pub about a bath.'

He was a large, jolly man, although a little downcast for the time being, since only the foolhardy and those who had had the flu and felt safe spent their evenings in the bar. 'But things will get better, Miss; bound to. You come across whenever you want. I'll show you where to go. Bring your own towel and soap, will you?'

He named a modest sum and Matilda, pleased with her arrangements, went home to pack a bag and promise to go home whenever she could. 'But I'll phone you each evening,' she assured her parents.

She decided to say nothing to the doctor; he had enough to worry about without bothering about her plans. And indeed she was right; he scarcely gave her a thought; his days were long and his nights short and frequently disturbed. True, he showed no signs of tiredness, he ate the meals put before him and his manner never varied from his usual calm. When he had occasion to speak to her it was in his usual polite, detached manner.

Matilda, aware that she was, as it were, invisible to him, didn't mind; just going there, helping him, was enough to go on with...

Mrs Trickett's cottage was lacking in mod cons but it was warm and Mrs Trickett herself was just as warm in her manner. Matilda, installed there by lunchtime took stock of her small bedroom and decided that she had been lucky. True, the room was very small but there was a thick old-fashioned quilt on the bed and, after all, she was only going to sleep there. She ate her midday dinner with Mrs Trickett in the kitchen, a nice piping hot stew and a pot of strong tea, and then went to the shop to buy groceries to take home with her on the following day. While Mrs Simpkins sliced bacon and weighed out the cheese, Matilda impressed upon her the need not to tell anyone that she was lodging with Mrs Trickett.

'You see, the doctor has so much to worry about at the moment, it would only bother him that I wasn't going home each day, but it's much easier for me to be close to the surgery now that it's so busy.'

Mrs Simpkins agreed. 'I'll not tell, miss. Reckon you're right not to bother the doctor more than he's bothered now.'

The flu was at its height; the very ill and elderly were taken to hospital whenever there was a bed but everyone else depended on Dr Lovell for antibiotics as well as resorting to old-fashioned remedies their grannies had used—the syrup from a Swede turnip sprinkled with sugar, camphorated oil, an old sock wrapped round the throat...!

It hadn't entered Matilda's head that she might get the flu too. In any case she was far too busy to think about it. A week went by and she went home twice with groceries, but not to stop. Her father she didn't see, judging it prudent in case she harboured germs, merely handing over what she had brought to her mother and going back to the village again. It was a blessing that they were on the phone and could keep in touch.

It was on Friday evening, after surgery, that Dr Lovell asked her if she would open the surgery on Saturday evening. It would give those who worked on the more distant farms a chance to come to the surgery, he explained, and he scarcely waited for her to agree.

And really, she reflected, she might just as well be there as sitting in Mrs Trickett's kitchen.

Saturday morning was as busy as usual for there were still the cut fingers, sprained ankles and aches and pains as well as the flu patients. Matilda closed the waiting-room door thankfully and, told to go into the surgery and have her coffee, went and sat down on the opposite side of the desk and lifted her mug of the fragrant brew. She put it down again as the door to the house was flung open.

Lucilla Armstrong stood there for a moment to allow any onlookers the chance to admire her. And indeed she was worth admiration; she was wearing a leather jacket, a very short skirt, suede boots to die for, and her fair hair was hanging in fashionable untidiness around her subtly made up face…

She said in a thrilling voice, 'Henry, darling, I knew you would be longing to see me so I drove straight from Heathrow.'

The doctor had got to his feet, and if he was surprised he didn't show it.

'Lucilla, this is unexpected…'

She came into the room, ignoring Matilda. 'I meant it to be. I didn't stop for anything, just got into the car and came here. I've had such a wonderful time.'

The doctor said quietly, 'Did you know that there's a flu epidemic in most of the country?'

'Flu? I haven't bothered with newspapers or the radio. Oh, Henry, it was delightful lying around in the sun all day…' She frowned. 'But there's no flu here?'

'Half the village is down with it. You should go home, Lucilla, and stay there until the epidemic is over.'

She was suddenly furious. 'Why didn't someone tell

me? I suppose this place is full of germs; I might even catch it just talking to you.'

'Possibly,' said Dr Lovell.

'And what is she doing here?' Lucilla nodded at Matilda.

Matilda answered before the doctor had a chance. 'She works here.'

She picked up her mug, went back into the waiting room and sat down at her desk, finishing her coffee. She took a look at the appointments book; the evening surgery would be full to overflowing. She hoped that the doctor would be back from his visits in time to open it promptly. It was likely to be a busy evening. She would go across to the pub and have a bath after her dinner and have tea with Mrs Trickett before coming back to work.

It was quiet and cold in the waiting room and although she couldn't hear voices she didn't like to go back into the surgery. When the doctor opened the door she looked up enquiringly.

'I'm off on my rounds. Mrs Inch doesn't feel well, so I've sent her to bed. Will you stay and take any messages? I've left my mobile phone number on my desk and I'll be back as soon as I can.'

He had gone before she could reply.

How like a man, thought Matilda, to walk out of his house and presently return to expect a cooked meal on the table, his slippers warmed by the fire, Sam taken for a walk and fed. She had to admit that wasn't quite fair; of course, he couldn't be expected to do otherwise and he had never spared himself. He must be tired, she thought lovingly, and went in search of Mrs Inch, who was lying on her bed and feeling very under the weather. She was fretting about who would get the doctor's meals and what about Sam and who was to answer the phone.

'Well, I will,' Matilda said cheerfully. 'You get into bed and I'll bring you a hot drink and you can tell me what must be done. Dr Lovell has asked me to stay until he gets back.'

'There's soup on the Aga,' said Mrs Inch as Matilda popped her nightgown over her head, 'and a chicken ready to go into the oven and an apple pie. Sam's food is in the cupboard by the door leading to the larder.'

She got gratefully into her bed. 'Doctor gave me some pills; I'll be on my feet in no time.'

'I'll bring you a drink and perhaps you'll be able to sleep. I won't bother you unless I must.'

Matilda sped downstairs and found the kitchen where Sam snoozed in his basket and a tabby cat was curled up on a chair by the Aga. Presently, when she had time, she would take a look round but now she was intent on finding milk and lemons and a small tray and glasses. That wasn't too difficult; it was the kind of kitchen where everything had a place and was in it.

Mrs Inch drank the hot milk, watched Matilda put the jug of lemonade within reach and closed her eyes thankfully, declaring again that she would be up and about in no time.

Matilda went back downstairs, let Sam into the garden, lunched hurriedly on soup and bread and butter and phoned Mrs Simpkins to ask her if she could let Mrs Trickett know that she wouldn't be back until the evening and then possibly late. 'Mrs Inch isn't well and I'm staying here to answer the phone until Dr Lovell gets back for evening surgery,' she explained.

There were several calls from those too ill to come to the surgery; she took names and addresses and hoped that the doctor wouldn't be too long away. Mrs Inch was asleep but she didn't look well, so Matilda went back downstairs and made a pot of tea and sat at the table drinking it. It was too early to put the chicken in the oven but she laid a tray with tea things, buttered some scones she found in the fridge, found bread and butter and a pot of Marmite and put them out ready to make sandwiches.

Both Sam and the cat were looking at her expectantly so she fed them. If they were going to be busy later they might be forgotten...

She glanced at the clock; there was still half an hour or so before evening surgery. She left the kitchen and went to explore the drawing room; she hadn't liked to stare too much when she had had her tea there, but now she could look her fill. She sat for a moment in a chair by the dying fire, allowing her thoughts to dissolve into daydreams. But not for long. She saw to the fire, put the fire guard back and went to the kitchen where she made the sandwiches, warmed the teapot and made sure that the kettle would boil in a moment. And by then it was time to open the surgery doors...

They were going to have a specially busy evening, she realised, explaining to the patients who came hurrying in that the doctor wasn't back. She got out their cards, wrote up her book and begged them to have patience before going back to the house to take a quick peep at Mrs Inch.

She had reached the hall when the doctor let himself in.

'Tea in a couple of minutes,' said Matilda briskly. 'I'm just going to take a look at Mrs Inch; there's a tray ready in the kitchen. The waiting room's full.'

She whisked herself upstairs and found Mrs Inch still

asleep and raced down again. The doctor was in the kitchen, eating the sandwiches, and she told him to sit down, made the tea, and while he was drinking it popped the chicken into the Aga. They didn't talk, for she saw that he was tired and hungry and he still had the surgery to cope with...

The doctor ate the last of the sandwiches and watched Matilda arranging saucepans on the Aga. She did it as though she had done it all her life and without any attempt to draw attention to herself. Strange to think that he hadn't been too keen on employing her; she was turning out to be a treasure. He had a fleeting vision of Lucilla dealing with the Aga with such efficiency and dismissed the idea as ludicrous; Lucilla was born to be a beautiful ornament for everyone to admire, to be cherished, spoilt, shielded from unpleasantness...

Matilda tucked a wisp of brown hair behind an ear. 'I'll check the waiting room,' she said, and left him alone.

The surgery ran well over its usual time but it had been a good idea; no one was seriously ill, and with good luck they would recover in their own homes provided they took care of themselves and took the antibiotics the doctor gave them.

Matilda locked the surgery door, tidied the room and after a moment's thought went into the surgery. The doctor was at his desk, coping with paperwork.

'I'll see to Mrs Inch,' said Matilda, 'and dish up your supper. Is anyone coming to help you in the morning?'

'No, I'll be quite all right, thank you, Miss Paige.'

'I dare say you will but Mrs Inch won't be. I'll come over about nine o'clock and see to her. Make the bed and so on. She won't want you to do it and she is not well enough to manage by herself.'

He looked at her then. She was quite right, of course. 'You must be needed at home. Your father is keeping well? Keeping away from the village?'

'Yes, he is very well. If you don't wish me to come in the morning then may I ask Mrs Simpkins to pop over? Mrs Inch would be upset...'

'Ah, yes, of course. Stupid of me. If your mother and father can spare you please come yourself, Miss Paige. I can manage very well now; you must wish to go home?'

'I'll just go up to Mrs Inch. Goodnight, Doctor.'

He was writing again. 'Goodnight, Miss Paige, and thank you.'

He didn't look up.

Mrs Inch was feeling more herself but she was glad of a little help, and to have her bed re-made, more lemonade, and a bowl of soup after a refreshing wash. Matilda had put the potatoes in the oven with the chicken and the parsnips and carrots were almost ready by the time she got downstairs. She set the kitchen table, put everything ready in the warm oven and found pencil and paper.

'Dinner ready to eat in the oven. Mrs Inch has had some soup and her pill. I hope you sleep well.'

She didn't sign it. Matilda was too familiar in the face of the doctor's detached coolness, Miss Paige sounded Gothic, so she scribbled her initials.

She would have to go out through the surgery; she knocked on the door and when there was no answer went in. He wasn't there. She went out through the waiting-room door, locking up after her.

Mrs Trickett had a hot meal ready for her, and then,

since it was a dark and cold evening, the good soul boiled up several kettles of hot water and left Matilda to have a good wash at the sink. It wasn't very satisfactory but she felt all the better for it, and presently, in her dressing gown, she went and sat in the kitchen with Mrs Trickett and dried her washed hair. It had been a long day and, pleasantly sleepy and further warmed by a cup of hot cocoa, Matilda went to bed. Before she slept she hoped that the doctor had eaten his supper and gone to bed too.

He had eaten his supper; he had gone to his study when Matilda had gone up to see Mrs Inch, but before long his splendid nose had caught an appetising whiff of something from the kitchen. Sam had got up from his place under the desk and gone to the door, and so had the doctor…

He had read Matilda's note first and then gone to the Aga. He'd been carving the chicken when he'd put down the carving knife and addressed Sam.

'I should have invited her to supper, driven her home at the very least; she must be asleep on her feet…'

He went upstairs to his housekeeper's room and found her awake.

'Miss Inch, did Miss Paige say that she was going home? She left the house while I was in my study.'

'Not home, sir. She's lodging with Mrs Trickett just across the street, so's to be on hand. Didn't want to take this nasty old flu home and Mrs Trickett's had it. Been there a couple of days. Don't say much about it—she's not one to do that—but Mrs Simpkins told me she's quite happy there. Mrs Trickett feeds her well and she nips across to the Lovell Arms for a bath.' She stopped to cough. 'Don't you worry about her, sir. A very capable young lady and everyone who knows her would help her.'

'Save myself, Mrs Inch,' said the doctor heavily.

'Lor' bless you, sir, you've enough on your plate keeping the rest of us on our feet. You go down and eat your supper and let's hope you'll get a good night's sleep.'

The chicken and everything that went with it was delicious; he tidied the kitchen and took Sam for an evening walk. He passed Mrs Trickett's house, suppressing an urge to knock on its door and ask to see Matilda. She was probably in bed and wouldn't thank him for a visit. Presently he went back home, and, tired though he was, dealt with the paperwork and the conditions of his ill patients. Then he went to bed and a kindly Providence allowed him to sleep all night.

CHAPTER FOUR

IT WAS a wet and cold Sunday morning. The pub wouldn't open until midday so there was no chance of going over for a bath. Matilda shared breakfast with Mrs Trickett, helped with the washing-up and then, well wrapped in her elderly mac, went across to the doctor's house.

She let herself in through the surgery waiting room and entered the hall, to be met by Sam and, a moment later, the doctor, coming out of the kitchen. She was happy to see that he looked rested and somehow much younger in cords and a thick sweater.

She wished him good morning and added, 'I've come to see to Mrs Inch if you don't mind?'

'Mind? My dear girl, I am beginning to think that I would be lost without you. Mrs Inch has told me that you have moved in with Mrs Trickett. You should have told me... And you cooked my supper.'

'No trouble,' said Matilda matter-of-factly. 'Everything was ready to put into the oven, and I'm very comfortable with Mrs Trickett. I didn't want to take the flu germs home and she's so handy, just across the street.'

'I'm grateful, Miss Paige. When you have seen Mrs Inch perhaps you will have coffee with me?'

'That'll be nice,' said Matilda, and nipped up the staircase.

Mrs Inch was no worse, but neither was she feeling much better. Matilda helped her to the bathroom lead-

ing from her bed-sitting room, put her into a clean
nightie, brushed her hair and tucked her into the freshly
made bed. 'A nice hot drink and some more lemonade,
then perhaps you can have a nap. Shall I pop over this
evening?'

'Would you? Just to freshen me up... Kitty will be
here in the morning. She's a good girl and quite a good
cook, and Mrs Squires will be in to do the rough.'

Matilda nipped downstairs, fetched the cup of tea
Mrs Inch craved and carried it back with the lemonade,
resisted the urge to tidy herself up before joining the
doctor—a waste of time anyway, she told herself, for
he wouldn't notice—and went back to the kitchen. He
was there and the coffee smelled delicious. He put their
mugs on the table, offered her a biscuit, gave one to
Sam and sat down opposite her.

'I am hopeful that we are over the worst,' he observed, 'with no new cases yesterday evening.'

'Oh, good; you must be very thankful. You won't
mind if I come this evening and see to Mrs Inch? She's
better, isn't she? But she doesn't feel up to doing
much.'

'I have not the least objection, Miss Paige. Perhaps
you will come in the late afternoon and share my tea?'

'All right,' said Matilda. 'If you want me to. Can
you manage to get your own lunch?'

'Thank you, yes.' He sounded so frosty that she
didn't ask about his supper. He had friends for that,
she was sure. They could be coming to get his supper
for him, and eat it with him too, no doubt. She finished
her coffee, put their mugs in the sink, bade him a civil
goodbye and started for the front door.

She reached the door, but he'd got there first.

'Just a moment, Miss Paige. Mrs Inch told me that

you go to the Lovell Arms for a bath. Not a very satisfactory arrangement. There are three bathrooms in
this house and an abundance of hot water. May I suggest you take advantage of that and have a bath here?'

Matilda eyed him thoughtfully. 'Now?'

'Why not? I shall be working in my study, Mrs Inch
appears to be comfortable and there is no one to hurry
you. If you go upstairs you will find a bathroom on the
right, the second door. Take as long as you like. No
need to tell me when you are ready to leave; the front
door is unlocked, so let yourself out.'

His offer had been made in a detached manner and
with the air of a man doing his duty, and Matilda, who
had been doubtful, allowed common sense to rule the
day.

'Thank you. That would be nice. I won't disturb anyone, doctor.'

He watched her go, wondering why on earth he had
suggested it. He went to his study, telling himself it
was an offer he would have made to anyone in similar
circumstances.

The bathroom was large, warm and well equipped.
Matilda lay in a steaming hot bath, lavishly scented
with something heavenly out of a bottle, and thought
about the doctor. She came to the conclusion that she
would never know what he was really like. She suspected that behind his austere manner there was quite
a different man lurking.

She washed her hair and then, swathed in a huge
soft bath towel, sat drying it. It was pleasant to sit there
in the lap of luxury, thinking about the doctor, and she
could have spent the rest of the morning doing just that,
but that, she felt sure, would be outstaying her wel-

come. She dressed and went quietly downstairs and let herself out into the quiet street.

She phoned her mother from the telephone box outside Mrs Simpkins's shop, assured her that she was well and hoped that she would be coming home as soon as the flu subsided. As she left the box Mrs Simpkins stuck her head out of an upstairs window.

'Bin over to the doctor's, love?'

'Yes, Mrs Simpkins, just to see to Mrs Inch. She's feeling a little better but doesn't feel like doing much; in fact, she's still in her bed. I'm going over again this afternoon, just to settle her. She said that someone called Kitty would be back tomorrow to look after her.'

'That'll be Kitty Tapper—housemaid, you might say. Going back to Mrs Trickett for your dinner?'

'Yes, Mrs Simpkins, and a nice quiet afternoon!'

Mrs Simpkins, thought Matilda, was a dear soul but did like to know everyone's business.

She ate her dinner with Mrs Trickett and then sat with her by the old-fashioned kitchen stove, reading the newspaper her companion shared with her. She had never read this particular tabloid before and its contents were startling enough to keep her engrossed.

She judged that half past four was the right time to go back to see to Mrs Inch, and the doctor opened the door to her, looking, for a moment, surprised to see her. He had his reading glasses on and held a sheaf of papers and she guessed that he had forgotten all about her.

'Shall I go and see how Mrs Inch is?' she suggested, sounding businesslike. 'And give her her tea before I see to her comfort?'

'Yes, yes, please do; you know where everything is.' He was already on his way back to his study.

Mrs Inch was awake, rather cross and longing for a cup of tea.

'I'll get it straight away,' Matilda promised, 'and then I'll make you comfortable. Do you feel a little better?'

'I suppose so. Dr Lovell has been in and out during the day. He says I'm on the mend. Very kind and thoughtful, he's been, and I know he's busy and men don't think about a cup of tea and suchlike, do they?'

'Well no,' agreed Matilda. 'I'll bring up a big pot and perhaps I can find a Thermos jug and leave it filled for you if you fancy a drink later on.'

'You're a very thoughtful young lady,' said Mrs Inch, 'and I believe I could manage a morsel of bread and butter cut thin.'

There was no sign of the doctor as she made tea and some wafer-thin slices of bread and butter, arranged everything neatly on a tray and took it back upstairs.

Mrs Inch, propped up on pillows, sipped her tea. 'That's a treat,' she observed. 'Now just you go down and have your tea with the doctor.'

A bit of a problem, decided Matilda, going down to a quiet house. Had he forgotten that he had asked her to tea? Or was she expected to get it for them both?

She found a tray and tea things, boiled the kettle and poked around the cupboards looking for cake or biscuits. There was a cake, or half of one. She put it on a plate and cut more bread and butter and went into the hall and looked doubtfully at the closed doors. Finally she tapped on the study door and went in.

The doctor was at his desk, writing, Sam at his feet.

He looked up as she went in, staring at her over his spectacles.

'Yes?' He sounded testy.

'Mrs Inch is quite comfortable until suppertime,' said Matilda baldly. 'Your tea is waiting for you in the kitchen.'

He frowned. 'Presently, presently. I have a good deal of writing to do.'

'I dare say you have. Go and have your tea now while it's still hot.'

She closed the door quietly after her and got into her coat and let herself out of the house. She was suddenly tired and dispirited. And, at the same time, cross. 'I hope he goes hungry to bed,' she muttered as she crossed the road to Mrs Trickett's cottage.

Even if the doctor didn't want his tea, Sam wanted his. He got up and wandered back and forth in doggy impatience until his master put down his pen and got up.

'All right, old fellow; we'll have tea and go for a walk. And I'd better look in on Mrs Inch.'

He ate all the bread and butter and most of the cake and drained the teapot while Sam ate a biscuit, then they both went up to Mrs Inch.

Mrs Inch assured him that she was feeling better. 'That Miss Paige made a lovely pot of tea and bread and butter; I couldn't have cut it thinner myself. Had your tea, have you, sir?'

'Yes, thank you, Mrs Inch. Miss Paige left it ready for me.' He stopped. 'Oh, God…'

Mrs Inch said severely, 'It's not like you to call upon the Lord, sir.'

'Mrs Inch, I asked Miss Paige to have tea with me when she came over this afternoon and I forgot. That's no excuse—I was working but I should have remembered. She got the tea and told me it was ready and left the house. Why didn't she remind me?'

Mrs Inch gave him an old-fashioned look. 'She'd rather go without her tea; she's not the pushy sort,' she said dryly.

'Mrs Inch, will you be all right if I go across and see her? Sam can have a quick run at the same time.'

'You do that, Doctor; I'm fine.'

It was drizzling as he let himself out of the house with Sam. It was Mrs Trickett who answered his knock.

'Doctor? Is something wrong? Do you want Miss Paige? Come in—and Sam...'

'Nothing is wrong, Mrs Trickett. If I might have a word with Miss Paige? You're keeping well? Quite recovered from the flu?'

Mrs Trickett led the way into the kitchen. 'Yes, thank you, Doctor. You don't mind the kitchen? It's warmer, and with just the two of us...'

'I think that the kitchen is sometimes the most cosy place in the house,' said the doctor. He paused in the doorway to look at Matilda, standing at the small sink, clasping a cabbage to her bosom like a shield.

She didn't put it down. She didn't say anything either, only looked at him unsmiling.

'Miss Paige, I've come to apologise. I invited you to have tea with me and forgot about you. Please forgive me?'

'Well, of course I do. I dare say you were too busy to think about it. Besides, I am the sort of person people forget.'

She spoke in a matter-of-fact voice with no trace of self-pity. It was merely a statement of a fact she had been aware of for years, first pointed out to her by her mother. She had accepted it as gospel truth without rancour but with regret.

Mrs Trickett had slipped away and the doctor came further into the small room, his head inches from the ceiling, his large person making it even smaller than it was.

'That's not true; take my word for it. Don't hide your light under a bushel, Miss Paige; I have come to regard you as indispensable.'

'I've done my best to follow in Miss Brimble's footsteps,' said Matilda.

He stared at her. She looked small and rather pale in the dim light of the single bulb, but not in the least sorry for herself. Indeed, she said tartly, 'There was no need for you to have come out…'

'Sam needed a run,' said the doctor meekly. 'I'll bid you goodnight and see you in the morning at the surgery.'

She went with him into the tiny hall and opened the door for him. It was a tight squeeze—him, her and Sam. At the door he turned to say, 'Please use my place for a bath; I'll tell Kitty you may be over during the day.'

'Thank you. Goodnight, Doctor.' She had a nice voice, he reflected, but still tart. There was more to Miss Matilda Paige than one would suppose.

The surgery was crowded in the morning; it was always the same on a Monday. The waiting room filled up, the air redolent of wet coats and a strong whiff of manure from the two farm workers, badly bruised by a slight mishap with a tractor. But it was heartening to find that there were no new flu patients.

The surgery ended late and the doctor went away

immediately. He had wished Matilda good morning in his usual detached manner, left her a couple of letters to answer and made no mention of a bath. She tidied up and got ready to leave, to be stopped by Kitty coming into the waiting room.

'If you don't mind coming into the kitchen, miss, there's coffee ready there. And Mrs Inch says could you look in on her before you have your bath. I've put out fresh towels for you.'

The coffee was hot and fragrant and Kitty was a friendly girl. Matilda drank it thankfully with Sam at her feet and Kitty sitting opposite her at the table. And presently she went to see Mrs Inch, who was sitting in a chair by the gas fire in her room.

'I'm better,' she declared, 'fit for work, but the doctor won't hear of it. Says I must take things easy for a day or two. I'm obliged to you, miss; you've been that good to me! Going to have a bath now? No one will disturb you so take your time; it's a sight better here than going over to the pub.'

Matilda agreed, listened to Mrs Inch's mild gossip for a few minutes then took herself off to the bathroom again. Sheer luxury, she reflected, lying in a foam-filled bath…

It was obvious that the worst of the flu epidemic was over; there were no new cases during the next few days and those who had been laid low were back on their feet. Matilda phoned home to say that she would be returning in a few days' time, and spent happy moments doing sums on any bit of paper handy. She had been paid overtime—the doctor had waved aside her objections to that—and she had had little chance to spend much money. Her mother would expect to have some of it and there were always unexpected or forgotten bills which her father had mislaid. Still, there would be enough over for her to go to Taunton again. A new mac, she decided, looking out of the window at the cold drizzle...

The waiting room was almost back to normal with its contingent of patients the next morning, for which Matilda felt thankful; she wasn't feeling as energetic as usual. A bit of a headache and a wish to climb into a warm bed somewhere and sleep. There wasn't time to think much about it, though; the doctor came punctually and the first of the patients went in. For once she found the surgery hours dragged; it seemed to her that he was being very slow that morning, which as it happened wasn't the case at all. It was only a short while after ten o'clock when she closed the door on the last patient and the doctor put his head round the surgery door.

'I'll see you this evening, Miss Paige,' he said, and nodded in a perfunctory manner and was gone.

Matilda sat down at the desk and began sorting patients' notes, but presently she laid her head down and closed her eyes. She really felt rather peculiar—hot and cold and aching. She sat up. This wouldn't do at all; she would go over to Mrs Trickett's and lie down for a while. She had a list of things her mother had asked her to bring with her and she would have to go to Mrs Simpkins' shop later.

She got to her feet, took a couple of steps and fell in an untidy heap.

Dr Lovell, back from his morning visits, returned Sam's enthusiastic greeting and went into the drawing room to open the doors so that they might both go into

the garden. It was a chilly day but dry and he stood
for a moment, enjoying the quiet and peace of it all.
The last few weeks had been tiring. Perhaps Miss Paige
would like a few days off; she had worked hard without
a single grumble.

He whistled to Sam and went to have his lunch, paid
a brief visit to Mrs Inch and got into his car again. The
flu epidemic might be on the wane but his practice was
wide-flung and with winter approaching there was always more illness.

He went to his study when he got back at around
four o'clock and then went to the surgery. And the first
thing he saw was the light shining under the waiting-
room door.

Matilda had woken up several times, aware that she
should get up, call for help, make some kind of a noise,
but it was too much trouble; she closed her eyes again
and prayed for her headache to go away. She had fallen
into another uneasy doze when the doctor opened the
door, but she roused at the sound of his voice.

She said weakly, 'Watch your language, Doctor,'
and then, 'I should like to sit down for a while—with
a hot-water bottle and a cup of tea.'

He didn't waste time on talk but scooped her up and
carried her out into the hall and up the staircase and
into one of the bedrooms, where he laid her on the bed,
took off her shoes and covered her with the quilt.

She lay looking at him, shivering, and he said gently,
'It's all right, Matilda; you've got the flu. Kitty will
come and help you to bed and I'll give you something
for that head.'

She stared at him with bright, feverish eyes; she felt
terrible but everything would be all right now. She
croaked an answer but he had already gone.

When she opened her eyes again Kitty was there, undressing her and shrouding her in one of Mrs Inch's nightgowns, and then it was the doctor again, bending over her, listening to her chest and sitting her up against her pillows while Kitty held her and told her to say ninety-nine.

She dozed then until Kitty came again with a cup of tea and a jug of lemonade. The doctor was there too; it was he who lifted her up again and held the cup to her mouth so that she could drink, and then, with a nod to Kitty, turned her gently and plunged a needle into her behind.

'Ow,' said Matilda, and two tears crept down her cheeks. He wiped them away and told her to go to sleep in a kind voice, and since staying awake wasn't too pleasant she closed her eyes.

They flew open again almost at once. 'You called me Matilda.'

'So I did,' said Dr Lovell, and laughed. A gentle, friendly laugh which sent her to sleep at once.

He stood looking down at her, half hidden in Mrs Inch's old-fashioned nightie. She was very pale and her hair was all over the pillow in an untidy tangle. Studying her face, he saw the delicately arched eyebrows and the curling eyelashes and felt surprise that he had never noticed them before. But of course he had never really looked at her. He had accepted her as a second Miss Brimble...

He went to see Mrs Inch then, and that lady tut-tutted and observed severely, 'Only to be expected, sir; the poor young lady's been on the go for two weeks or more and never a grumble from her. I shall come down tomorrow and sit in the kitchen. Kitty can manage if I'm there to tell her what's what and it's Mrs Murch's day for the rough cleaning. And who's to manage the surgery for you?'

'Oh, I can see to myself, Mrs Inch. If you come downstairs I must insist that you stay in the kitchen and do nothing. You think that Kitty can manage?'

'Lor' bless you, sir, of course she can, and she'll look after Miss Paige a treat.'

'Thank you, Mrs Inch. I'm going to phone Mrs Paige; she might have some suggestions of her own.'

But when presently he suggested to Matilda's mother that she might like to visit her daughter—stay in his house for a few days and look after her if she wished—he was met with a flurry of excuses.

'But I might get the flu,' objected Mrs Paige. 'I am so delicate, Doctor, that the least breath of infection would have severe consequences. Matilda will be on her feet again in no time; she is really very healthy. I know she doesn't look much…' When the doctor said nothing, she went on hurriedly, 'What I mean is that she's small and doesn't look strong… Should she go to hospital? I really can't have her home.'

'No, Mrs Paige.' His voice was detached, professional. 'She isn't well enough to move and in any case I wouldn't think of doing that. Mrs Inch will look after her and I shall of course treat her with antibiotics and make sure that she is fit for work again.'

'Oh, Doctor, that would be splendid. Give her my love, please, and we shall be glad to have her home once she is well again.'

He put down the phone and stood thinking for a moment then dialled another number.

'Mother? I have a small problem; is Aunt Kate still with you? She is? Do you suppose she would care to stay for a few days here with me? It's like this…'

He put the phone down presently and went in search of Mrs Inch.

She listened to what he had to say and nodded with approval. 'Miss Paige is a clergyman's daughter and a proper young lady. We don't want her worrying, do we? When will Miss Lovell be coming?'

'Some time tomorrow afternoon; she will drive over.'

'Well, that's settled, sir. Miss Paige isn't one to lie about doing nothing. I dare say she'll be on her feet and away the moment she's fit.'

'But not before I say she may,' said Dr Lovell.

Later that evening he went to see how Matilda was and found her awake and not well enough to care two pins where she was or why. Which saved a great deal of explaining. He dosed her with an antibiotic, gave her a drink and turned her pillow. She said in a small, hoarse voice, 'Thank you, I'm very comfortable now,' and dozed off.

But last thing that night as he was going to bed he took another look at her and found her hot and restless. Mrs Inch was long a-bed and so was Kitty; he bathed her hot face, gave her a drink, pulled a chair up to the bed and took a hand in his.

'Don't go,' said Matilda. 'I don't feel very well...'

'I know, but I promise you will feel much better tomorrow. Close your eyes and go to sleep and if you wake in the night just call out. I shall hear.'

'You're a different you!' said Matilda, voicing a thought from the chaos inside her poor head and presently falling into a deep sleep.

She woke early and the doctor was there giving her a pill and a long cool drink, then she slept again. When

she woke for the second time it was to find Kitty, mur-
muring in a comforting voice and proffering tea. And
it was Kitty who washed her face and hands and put
her into another of Mrs Inch's nightgowns.

She was asleep again when the doctor came to see
her after the morning surgery but later, when she
roused, it was to find Mrs Inch, dressed in a dressing
gown but looking almost her normal self, bending over
her.

'I'm being a great nuisance,' said Matilda. She
would have said more but her headache was still trou-
blesome. She drank the lemonade she was offered and
closed her eyes again. But not to sleep; she hadn't felt
well enough to bother about being where she was, but
now the thought that she was in the doctor's house,
making a nuisance of herself, began to bother her. A
few tears crawled down her cheeks but she couldn't be
bothered to wipe them away and presently she dozed
off.

When she opened her eyes again the doctor was
looming over her, to be replaced by an elderly face
with a beaky nose and crowned by white hair.

'I'm Aunt Kate,' said the owner of the hair, 'come
to stay with my nephew Henry. And you, child, are
Matilda?'

Matilda nodded. 'But please go away. I've had the
flu and you mustn't get it.'

'Bless the child, I never catch anything—ask Henry.'

The idea of asking the doctor any such thing struck
Matilda as amusing. She said in a polite, tired little
voice, 'I hope you will enjoy your stay with the doctor.' She allowed her thoughts to spin into words. 'He
must be glad to have you; he's been so busy—he must
be very tired and he never complains, you know.' She

rambled on, 'He's kind and he makes you feel safe, if you see what I mean, even if he doesn't like you very much.'

Aunt Kate's blue eyes narrowed but all she said was, 'Yes, you're so right. Now I'm going away to have my tea and presently someone will bring you tea and some bread and butter. You're feeling better, child.'

She spoke with such conviction that Matilda indeed felt better.

Aunt Kate found the doctor in his study, on the phone. She sat down and listened to the one-sided conversation and when he put the phone down said, 'Who was that, Henry? You sounded very smooth.'

'Mrs Paige—Matilda's mother.'

'Indeed—then why isn't she here with her daughter?'

'She is anxious not to get the flu.' The doctor sounded bland. 'She has told me that she has a delicate constitution.'

'Pooh,' said Aunt Kate. 'I mustn't ask any questions, must I, if she's one of your patients? Has the child a father?'

'Oh, yes, a delightful man, retired after a severe heart attack, has to take life easily. A clergyman.'

'And Matilda?'

'Their only child and I know very little about her, Aunt Kate; she is a quiet girl with a sharp tongue at times. Very efficient and hard-working.'

'And certainly no beauty,' said Aunt Kate. 'No boyfriend?'

'I have no idea.' The doctor frowned. The idea of Matilda having a boyfriend rankled.

It was two days before Matilda felt better but by no means well. She had taken her pills, swallowed drinks and done her best to eat the tasty small dishes Mrs Inch cooked for her, dimly aware of the doctor's visits and the frequent visits from Aunt Kate, urging her to drink this or eat that, or go to sleep. And sometimes it was Mrs Inch or Kitty bending over her, washing her, changing her nightie. She should be worrying about something, she thought fretfully, but it was too wearying to do so.

On the third morning, though, she woke with a clear head, aware that she really was feeling better. She told the doctor so when he came to see her before he went to the surgery and he studied her pale face and agreed that of course she was; another day or two and she would be out of bed, feeling quite her old self. She ate her breakfast with the beginnings of a good appetite, sitting up in bed so that she could see out of the window. For November it was a fine day, with a washed-out blue sky and thin sunshine.

'It's going to be a lovely day,' said Matilda when Aunt Kate came to visit her.

And it was until Kitty went to answer the door after lunch and Lucilla swept past her.

She was in a rage and prepared to vent it upon anyone. It was a pity that Mrs Simpkins, enjoying a gossip with her sister who lived in the village of North Curry where Lucilla's family lived, should have mentioned Matilda's illness and that she was being cared for at the doctor's home. The news had reached Lucilla's ears quickly enough and she'd lost no time in driving to Much Winterlow to see for herself.

She addressed Kitty in peremptory tones. 'What's all this talk of that girl staying here in the house? Where's the doctor? Why wasn't I told?'

Kitty backed away. 'The doctor's away on his rounds, miss, and Miss Paige is lying sick upstairs...'

'Of all the nonsense—she should be sent to hospital. Why hasn't she gone home? She has one, presumably? I shall wait for the doctor.'

She pushed past Kitty and flung open the drawing-room door.

'Come in—Lucilla, isn't it?—and sit down,' said Aunt Kate. 'You seem upset. Henry won't be back for some time but I'm sure you will stay a little while and have a cup of tea with me presently.'

Lucilla said, 'Miss Lovell—I didn't expect to find you here. I heard some tale about Henry's receptionist being here...'

'Indeed she is—very ill with flu; too ill to move. How fortunate that I was visiting Henry and have been able to look after her. There has been such a lot of flu about, hasn't there? It is most kind of you to come all this way to ask after her.'

'Yes, well...has she no home to go to?'

'Her parents live in the village but she has a semi-invalid father and I understand that her mother is very delicate.'

Aunt Kate fell silent, knitted a row of the garment she was working on and added gently, 'Such a hard worker; I'm told that she was a great help to Henry during these last difficult weeks. Such a pity that after helping so many people she should have been struck down herself.'

Lucilla said, 'Oh, yes,' in an insincere voice and Aunt Kate, glancing at her with bright blue eyes, decided that she definitely didn't like the girl. Beautiful, but no heart, she decided silently, and began a series of polite enquiries about Lucilla's family. She didn't much care for her family either; it would be a disastrous marriage if she managed to get Henry to the altar. Aunt Kate reflected thankfully that Henry was no fool; he had been attracted to Lucilla—after all, she was a beautiful young woman—but he would want more than beauty in the girl he chose to marry.

Aunt Kate heaved a sigh and hoped that Kitty would have the good sense to bring the tea tray without being asked to do so. Mrs Inch would still be having her afternoon nap and Kitty might be busy in the kitchen and not notice the time.

The door opened and Kitty came in, set the tray down on the small table by Aunt Kate and assured her that she would take tea upstairs to Miss Paige when she went to rouse Mrs Inch.

Aunt Kate poured tea, offered cake, and polite small talk, and wished that Henry would return. But there was no sign of him and presently Lucilla said, 'I won't stay; Henry will probably be late and the evenings are so dark for driving. May I go and tidy myself…?'

'Of course, Lucilla. You know where the cloakroom is, don't you?'

Lucilla smiled and went out of the room but not to the cloakroom. She ran silently up the staircase and opened doors just as silently until she opened the door into the dimly lit room where Matilda was in bed. She had been asleep but turned her head and half sat up as the door opened to stare at Lucilla. She said in a still hoarse voice, 'Hello. It's Miss Armstrong, isn't it?'

Lucilla came and stood by the bed. She said in a satisfied voice, 'You look frightful; you're not exactly eye-catching when you are on your feet but now you look like a washed-out hag.' She laughed. 'And to think I was worried…!'

She had gone again before Matilda could say anything. But what was there to say anyway? She didn't cry often but now the tears welled up and she let them trickle down her cheeks. If she was a washed-out hag what would a few tears matter?

CHAPTER FIVE

LUCILLA reached the hall just as the doctor let himself into his house. 'Lucilla—what brings you here?' If she had expected delighted surprise she was to be disappointed. He glanced at the staircase behind her, his eyebrows raised in an unspoken question. 'Aunt Kate is in the drawing room?'

Lucilla said hurriedly, 'Yes, I've had tea with her—just a passing visit; I hoped you might be here.'

He said quietly, 'You went to see Matilda?'

'Is that her name? Yes. The poor thing, she does look ill. She must be so thankful to be well looked after.'

He didn't answer her, merely opened the drawing-room door for her to go in then closed it behind her and went up the staircase, two at a time.

Tears hardly added to Matilda's wan looks. When she saw who it was she blew her small red nose, mopped her eyes and said politely, 'Good evening, Doctor.'

He ignored this poor attempt at polite small talk. 'You are upset. Lucilla came to see you, did she not? And what had she to say?'

Matilda sniffed. 'Just—well, you know, the usual things you say to someone when they're not well.'

'No. I don't know, Matilda. Enlighten me?'

He sat down on the side of the bed and took one of her hands in his. It was large and cool and comforting. 'Well?'

86

She gulped. 'I expect I look awful.' And then she added, 'It was very kind of Miss Armstrong to come and see me. I hope I haven't given her any germs.'

'No, no. The worst is over; you'll be on your feet in a couple of days.' Which wasn't quite true but she needed bolstering up. 'Several people have asked how you are; you have any number of friends in the village, you know.'

'Have I? I'm happy here…' She tugged gently at her hand and he let it go at once. 'I expect you want to go downstairs and talk to Miss Armstrong; she came specially to see you.'

He got up, looking down at her with a faint smile. 'Yes, she and I will have a talk. Are you quite comfortable? Do you want Kitty for anything?'

She shook her head. 'I've everything I want,' she told him, reflecting that she would never have that for everything was the doctor, wasn't it?

Aunt Kate looked up as he went into the drawing room and Sam went to greet him with a waving tail and a happy bark or two. Only Lucilla avoided his look and said nothing.

The doctor sat down, accepted the tea Kitty had brought in and began to talk pleasantly about nothing in particular until Lucilla, at first uncertain as to what he might say about her visit to Matilda, joined in and, sure of her charm and attraction, began to talk about their various friends and acquaintances. She was a clever talker and amusing, but not always kind in her comments. Her companions listened with polite interest and presently the doctor got up.

'Time for surgery,' he observed, and thought what a very handsome young woman Lucilla was, sitting there, smiling and now completely at her ease. She was looking at him with smiling expectancy and he had a sudden remembrance of Matilda's tear-stained face. He went to the door. His, 'Goodbye, Lucilla,' was cool and he made no mention of further meetings.

Aunt Kate picked up her knitting once more, looking composed. Henry, she reflected, was no more in love with Lucilla than she herself was. He might have been attracted to her when they'd first met and on the surface she seemed to have everything a man would want in a wife. And she had been clever, saying all the right things at the right time, a pleasant companion, a good-looking, elegant young woman, apparently interested in his work, allowing him to know that she more than liked him but never demonstrating it. Henry wasn't a man to be hurried but she was content to bide her time. He was a man worth waiting for: from a deeply re-spected family, with wealth, good looks, a splendid home and a host of influential friends. That he was also a highly qualified medical man was only of secondary interest. Quite unsuitable, decided Aunt Kate.

She went up to see Matilda presently, took one look at her unhappy face, pulled up a chair close to the bed and observed,

'You're upset. I dare say Lucilla said something to make you so downcast?'

'I'm sure she didn't mean to,' said Matilda, who, being a clergyman's daughter, did her best to see good in everybody. 'And it was quite true.'

'What was?' said Aunt Kate, and her beaky nose quivered slightly but her voice was gentle.

'Well, I'm sure that I do look like a washed-out hag, only I'd rather not be told.' She was silent for a moment then said, 'Miss Lovell, I would like to go home. I'm really much better and I'll be quite all right—if I just have a few days off I could come back to work again quite soon.'

Aunt Kate said decisively, 'Henry won't allow that.'

'No, well, I didn't think he would, but if you could persuade him? He told me that I would be well in a couple of days.'

'There is a difference between being well and being fit for work,' said Aunt Kate. 'I understand that your mother is delicate. Would she be able to cosset you? Breakfast in bed and making sure that you spent your days being lazy?'

'Oh, but I shall be fine once I'm home,' said Matilda in a cheerful voice which belied her seedy appearance. 'Please, Miss Lovell.'

'I will promise nothing, my dear, but if Henry should mention the matter I will see what I can do.'

An answer which hardly held much promise but which Matilda found reassuring enough.

Aunt Kate went down to the drawing room presently and when the doctor joined her after the surgery was finished she voiced the thoughts she had been mulling over.

'Matilda wishes to go home, Henry.'

He had gone to pour their drinks. 'Well, she can't; she's not fit.'

He sat down in his great chair with Sam at his feet. 'Why?'

His aunt took a sip of sherry. 'I hesitate to say this, Henry, for I am sure from what Lucilla says that you and she... Anyway, she upset Matilda so that the child feels she must go away.'

'What did she say? Lucilla is sometimes a little sharp. I know that you wouldn't tell me unless you thought it might help the matter.'

'She told Matilda that she was a washed-out hag.
You may not know this, but Matilda knows that she is
a plain girl and a remark such as that, even if it were
meant jokingly, is discouraging to someone not in the
best of health.' Aunt Kate gave him a thoughtful look.
'And I think, from what she has told me, that there is
little chance of her being looked after adequately at
home. She is very loyal towards her mother but it is
obvious that she can expect very little attention.'

'Then she must stay here until she is quite well.'

'I have an idea,' said Aunt Kate briskly. 'I shall be
delighted to take her home with me for a few days,
and when she is quite her usual self she can come back
to work. I shall leave it to you to speak to her parents
but I imagine her mother will agree without a moment's hesitation.'

'Oh, without doubt. You are sure that Matilda wishes
to go away from here?' He frowned. 'Why?'

'Yes, dear, and I will tell you why. She neither feels
nor looks her best—she wants to go somewhere and
hide until she is once more your efficient receptionist.'

He said slowly, 'If you think that is what she would
like we will get her on her feet in a few days and you
can take her home with you. Indeed, it is a most sensible idea provided you won't find it too much of a
bother?'

'No. I shall enjoy her company. You will take her
back?'

The doctor looked astonished. 'Of course. She is a
splendid worker; I don't know how I would have managed without her.' He smiled suddenly. 'Besides, she
is very restful in her ways and always there when I
want her. One hardly notices her and yet she is always
there when she is needed.'

Aunt Kate was glad to know that Matilda couldn't hear him say that...

Matilda, much encouraged by the prospect of going to stay with Aunt Kate, began to recover, and two days later the doctor declared that she was fit enough to leave his house. Something she was glad to do; shut away in a bedroom with only his two official visits each day had been one thing, but on her feet once more, sitting with Aunt Kate, sharing their meals, she was seeing too much of him for her own peace of mind. She had phoned her mother and since Mrs Paige had declared herself to be feeling poorly Kitty had gone to fetch Matilda some more clothes. She had no idea where Aunt Kate lived but wherever it was it must merit her tweed suit and the blue wool crêpe dress, out of date and seldom worn but entirely suitable in a face-less kind of way for most occasions.

She was surprised to discover that Aunt Kate had her own car, an elderly Jaguar, beautifully maintained and, to Matilda's eye, hardly suitable for someone of her advanced years to drive. But the doctor, seeing them off after morning surgery, seemed to find nothing strange about it; he even forbore from telling his aunt to drive carefully.

Apart from telling her that she lived near Somerton, Aunt Kate hadn't volunteered any more information and Matilda didn't wish to appear inquisitive. That part of Somerset was more or less new to her and she saw quickly enough that they were taking narrow lanes across country and that Aunt Kate drove with the non-chalant ease of a young man. They reached Hatch Beauchamp, drove on to Langport and then turned off the main road to Somerton, into another narrow lane bearing the signpost to High Ham.

The village, a mile or so ahead, was easy to see, perched on top of a hill, queening it over the surrounding flat countryside. And the village itself, when they reached it, was a delight to the eye with old houses gathered round a green and a splendid church alongside. There were one or two shops, a butcher, baker, village stores and post office, and Aunt Kate said as she swept past, 'We can get all we want here but there are shops at Somerton, only a few miles away.'

She drove down a lane between the houses and stopped before a handsome wrought-iron gate. 'The garage is at the end of the lane; we'll go into the cottage first.'

It was a very different cottage from Matilda's home, built of honey-coloured stone, its slate roof overgrown with moss. The last of the Virginia creeper which covered its walls had long since lost its leaves; in the summer it would be a picture. The windows were small and diamond-paned and its solid wood door would withstand a siege.

Aunt Kate produced a large old-fashioned key from her handbag and opened the door and urged Matilda past her into the hall. It was delightfully warm and through an open door she could see a bright fire burning.

'Mrs Chubb?' called Aunt Kate, and an elderly woman came through the door at the back of the hall.

'There you are, ma'am.' She shot a glance at Matilda. 'And the young lady. There's a good fire burning in the sitting room and there'll be lunch in half an hour. I'll fetch in the bags...'

'Later will do, Mrs Chubb. You'll be going home

presently so wait until you've got your coat on. It's cold this morning.'

'I've put out the sherry and Taffy's by the fire,' said Mrs Chubb comfortably, and withdrew to the kitchen.

'I'll show you your room,' said Aunt Kate. 'Come down again without waste of time, Matilda; we can unpack later on.'

She led the way up a narrow straight staircase to the square landing above and opened one of the doors there. The room was a fair size with a sloping roof and a pretty flowery paper on its walls. The furniture was painted white and there was a thick carpet underfoot and a patchwork quilt on the bed; the bedside lamps had pink shades and there were books, a biscuit tin and a tiny nosegay of violets on one of the bedside tables.

'The bathroom is next door, my dear, but do come down as soon as you're ready.'

Matilda, left alone, stood looking around her. The room was delightful; she knew that she would sleep peacefully in it and getting up in the morning would be a joy. And perhaps here she would be able to come to terms with herself, face the fact that to the doctor she was no more than someone who worked for him, someone whom he had considered it his duty to look after when she got the flu. He had been kind and concerned for her but it was Lucilla he intended to marry and she could quite understand why—any man would fall in love with those blonde good looks.

'But she won't make him happy,' Matilda told her pasty reflection as she powdered her nose. 'She's spiteful and most unkind. Not to him, of course...'

She went downstairs and went rather shyly into the sitting room. Aunt Kate was there, sitting by the fire, a large ginger cat curled up on her lap.

'Come in, child. As you can see I can't get up with Taffy already asleep. He is so glad to have me home again. Will you pour us both a sherry? Come and sit down by the fire. You like your room?'

'It's charming, and what a big garden you have—I looked out of the window.'

'I enjoy gardening. Bob from the village does all the hard work, of course. And whenever Henry comes he advises me. He has rather a splendid garden behind his house. I dare say you've seen it?'

'Only briefly. I usually go in through the waiting-room door and leave the same way.'

'A lovely old place; you must get him to show you round it some time.'

A remark which needed only a polite murmur in response.

They lunched together presently: homemade vegetable soup, cheese omelettes, warm rolls and farm butter. Aunt Kate drank mineral water but Matilda was given a glass of milk.

'You need fattening up, child,' said Aunt Kate.

'That she does,' observed Mrs Chubb, removing plates. 'Thin as a sparrow and washed out. Nasty thing, this flu.' She beamed at them both. 'Send you back with colour in your cheeks, we will, won't we?'

'We will indeed, Mrs Chubb.'

It was impossible not to get better, reflected Matilda a few days later. On the one hand there was Aunt Kate, taking her for brisk walks, well wrapped up so that she went back to the house glowing, to spend happy hours going round the cottage with her hostess, looking at its treasures: its antique furniture, the silver displayed in the little bow-fronted cabinet, the paintings of long-dead Lovells on the walls.

'Of course Henry has most of them,' said Aunt Kate, 'and his mother has a very nice collection.'

Matilda wondered where that lady lived but didn't like to ask.

And on the other hand Mrs Chubb was determined to do her part in sending Matilda back a credit to her splendid cooking. Between the two ladies Matilda blossomed into pink-cheeked plumpness. She had been there for five happy days when she said, 'Miss Lovell, I love being here but I'm quite well again and I ought to go back to work. And Mother must be needing me at home; she's had to manage by herself for too long.'

Aunt Kate's beaky nose quivered—another woman would have sniffed.

'I am loath to let you go, Matilda. Henry suggested that you should stay a week and I respect his judgement. So we will enjoy another two days together, my dear. And now that you feel quite recovered I thought that we might go to Somerton tomorrow—there are one or two shops there and you have had no chance to spend your money. We might see a pretty dress. You always look nice, but one can never have enough clothes at your age.'

There was money in Matilda's purse: two weeks' wages and the overtime money that the doctor had insisted on paying her. She said now, 'I need a new raincoat...'

'No, Matilda,' said Aunt Kate decisively, 'you need a pretty dress. Sooner or later Mr Right, as my nanny always called him, will come along, and although he will certainly love you in a shabby mackintosh you will want to look your best.'

'I don't know any Mr Right!' said Matilda.

'That's what makes life so exciting—never knowing if he may be round the next corner.'

'Well,' said Matilda., 'if I see something I like…'

They went the next morning and after they had had coffee in a stylish little café Aunt Kate led the way to a boutique in a lane just off the main street.

'Henry's sisters often go here,' she told Matilda. 'Don't look at the prices in the window; there's a splendid selection of clothes inside at most reasonable prices.'

She led the way in and was met by a stout little woman who wished them good morning. She and Aunt Kate had had an interesting conversation already that morning and since Aunt Kate was a good customer she had agreed to alter the price tickets if the young lady decided to buy anything.

And, taking a look at Matilda's good tweed suit, not only out of date but not warm enough for the time of year, she could see that new clothes were a necessity.

'I want a dress,' said Matilda. 'Something that won't go out of date too soon, something I could wear for a formal occasion.' Was meeting Mr Right a formal occasion? she wondered, and smiled at the thought so that the sales lady decided that, properly dressed, she would look pretty…

There was a splendid choice and well within her budget. She chose a silk jersey top and skirt in a deep pink which gave her mundane features a glow, and, since she was assured that it was half price as it was a small size and unlikely to sell easily, she allowed herself to be helped into a winter coat. It was grey and of a slightly military cut, and had, said the sales lady, been bought by a customer who had decided that she didn't like it once she got it home. Since it had been worn once, it would have to be sold at a very reduced price or go into the January sale. So if the young lady didn't mind?

The young lady was delighted. True, she was almost penniless, but she had been paying in most of her wages into her father's account and as far as she knew there were no big bills outstanding.

They left the shop presently and took the dress boxes to the car.

'What marvellous luck,' said Matilda. 'It's like a miracle, Miss Lovell.'

And worth every penny, reflected Aunt Kate, looking at Matilda's happy face.

They had lunch at a hotel in the main street and then spent a short time looking in the shop windows. And in one of the small shops there was exactly the hat to go with the new coat. And that accounted for the last money in Matilda's purse. But there would be another pay day in a week's time, and if her mother needed anything Christmas wasn't so far off; there would be presents to buy...

They went back to the cottage for tea and Matilda displayed her new clothes to Mrs Chubb, delighted to be told that she looked a fair treat.

They went for a walk the next morning because she wanted one more look at the country round her. It was unlikely that she would visit Miss Lovell again; she had loved every minute of her stay with the two elderly ladies, and their kindness and gentle spoiling and cheerful talk. She would miss Taffy too, for after a cautious day or so he had become her firm friend.

They spent the afternoon round the fire after Matilda had phoned her mother to tell her that she would be

home the next day. Mrs Paige had sounded peevish and
expressed the hope that Matilda would settle down to
a normal life once more. Matilda had gone to her room
to pack then, wishing with all her heart that she weren't
leaving in the morning.

She had asked hesitantly how she was to return and
when Aunt Kate had said that she would take her
Matilda had suggested that she might get a bus. It
would be an awkward journey as she would have to
change at Taunton but that was preferable to Aunt Kate
wasting a morning taking her back. But Aunt Kate
shook her head at the idea. 'Besides, I want to see
Henry again.'

So after breakfast Matilda put on the new coat and
hat and went along to the kitchen to say goodbye to
Mrs Chubb and give her the scarf she had bought for
her. She was hugged and kissed for it and told to be a
good girl and not to work too hard. She went in search
of Aunt Kate and gave her the little china figure they
had both admired in a shop at Somerton; she made her
thank-you speech too because there might not be a
chance to do that once they got back to Much
Winterlow. She was hugged and kissed once more and
only then noticed that Aunt Kate was still without her
hat and coat, but before she had time to ask about that
the door opened and Dr Lovell came in.

His good morning was genial; he kissed his aunt and
then turned to study Matilda.

'Ah—our Miss Paige, fully restored to good health,'
he observed. 'You feel quite well?'

So she was to be Miss Paige once more. The warm
friendliness while she had been ill had been temporary.
She said woodenly, 'Yes, thank you, Doctor; I feel
quite well again.'

As indeed she was, nicely plumped out and with a pretty colour in her cheeks. The doctor had seen the coat and the fetching little hat too. She looked pretty, but not as pretty as when she had been sweeping up leaves in some shapeless garment with her hair blowing all over the place.

'You must have coffee before you go,' said Aunt Kate into the silence, and expertly on cue Mrs Chubb came in with the coffee tray.

'Oh,' said Matilda, 'but I thought I was going back with you, Miss Lovell?'

She sounded so disappointed that the doctor said quickly, 'I'm afraid you will have to put up with me. You would like to go straight home, I expect?'

'Yes, please. It's very kind of you to take me.' She added anxiously, 'I'm not wasting your morning?'

'Not at all. ' He sounded casually polite. His morning, he reflected, was something he had been looking forward to.

'Have you seen anything of Lucilla?' asked Aunt Kate.

'No. No, I haven't.' He hadn't thought about her either. 'I've been quite busy; the flu's over but it is quite a busy time of year. I've been lucky enough to borrow a nurse from the Taunton health centre but she can't wait to get back there.' He smiled at Matilda. 'We have all missed you and I'm sure your mother and father will be delighted to have you home again.'

Matilda said politely, 'Yes, I think they will,' and fell silent for lack of anything else to say. Then, after a pause, she added, 'I shall be glad to come back to work.'

'And we shall all be glad to see you again.'

They left presently and since the doctor didn't seem

disposed to talk Matilda sat beside him and didn't utter a word. It didn't take long to reach Much Winterlow, which in the circumstances was a good thing.

He drove straight through the village and along the road to the cottage, and if Matilda had expected a warm welcome she didn't get it.

Her mother met them at the door. 'You didn't do any shopping on the way?' she asked crossly. 'There's nothing much in the house. You'll have to go this afternoon.'

Mrs Paige became all at once charming. 'Forgive me, Doctor, but my nerves are quite shattered. I've struggled along somehow but I'm exhausted.'

She led the way into the sitting room. 'Your father's in the study. You had better go and see him, Matilda. Doctor, come and sit down. It will be a treat for me to have someone to talk to.'

He followed her into the room and sat down. A tiresome woman, selfish to the bone; he had seen Matilda's face and it had left him strangely disquieted.

'Mr Paige keeps well?' he asked.

'Oh, yes. As long as he has his books and his writing he is happy.' Mrs Paige gave a sigh. 'He is a good deal older than I.' Her smile held a calculated wistfulness. 'I do miss the busy social life I had...'

'You will find that there is plenty of social life in the village. And you can safely go there now the flu is over.'

He stood up as Matilda came into the room. 'If your mother needs some shopping done you had better come back with me.'

Which made sense. Matilda nodded. 'Thank you. What do you want me to buy, Mother?'

Her mother said peevishly, 'Everything. There's almost nothing in the house; I knew you would be back today.' She added, 'You'll have enough money with you…'

'No, I haven't.' Matilda looked guilty, thinking of the coat and dress she had bought, and as though her mother had read her thoughts she said, 'Well, not surprising, I suppose. You've spent it all on yourself.'

Matilda had gone very pink in the face, aware of the doctor standing there. She said, 'If you could give me a list and some money, Mother.'

She didn't look higher than the doctor's waistcoat. 'Please don't wait; the walk to the shop will be pleasant after sitting in the car.'

The pink got deeper. 'What I mean is—the car's most comfortable, I enjoyed the drive and thank you for bringing me, but I'm sure you must want to get home…'

He took pity on her. 'It's my day off and I have nothing to do but please myself. So we will go back to the village and if your mother can spare you for an hour or so you must have a word with Mrs Inch and Kitty.'

'I've no time to make a list,' said Mrs Paige crossly. 'You'll have to bring whatever you can think of.'

She took money from her handbag. 'And bring the receipt back.'

Matilda could think of nothing to say as they drove back to Mrs Simpkins's shop. The doctor had got out and opened the door before she had a chance to do it. He went into the shop with her too and wandered around looking at the shelves while she made her purchases. The money her mother had given her wouldn't go far—tea and sugar, butter, streaky bacon and eggs, a tin of the cheapest salmon, cheese, macaroni.

Matilda, after totting everything up in her head, added
a packet of biscuits. There was just enough money over
for three lamb chops.

Mrs Simpkins kept up a cheerful flow of talk as she
assembled the food, but that didn't prevent the doctor,
who had excellent hearing, from knowing exactly what
Matilda had bought.

There was something wrong somewhere, he reflected. Mr Paige would have a pension, surely, and he
must have received some kind of financial assistance
when he'd retired, or at least had capital of some sort.
Obviously it was necessary for Matilda to get a job so
that she might be independent of her parents, but it
looked as though she was the breadwinner. And, now
he came to think about it, Mrs Milton had mentioned
one day that Mrs Paige put them all to shame at the
bridge afternoons. 'So smart,' she had explained in her
kind voice. 'But of course she has good clothes—I admire a woman who takes such pains with her appearance. And that costs money but her husband is devoted
to her and she lacks for nothing. So nice to see in a
middle-aged couple, don't you think?'

He hadn't thought much about it at the time but now
he frowned down at a stack of washing powder. It was
none of his business, of course, but it seemed to him
that Matilda was entitled to spend every penny she
earned on herself if she wished to do so. And heaven
knows, he thought wryly, the girl's got no looks to
speak of and a little pampering would be an improvement.

He looked at her now, stowing groceries into plastic
bags. There was no sign of the happiness he had seen
on her face that morning at Aunt Kate's. But neither
was there discontent. She might not be a beauty but he

had to admit there was something very restful about Matilda.

He took the bags from her, bade Mrs Simpkins good day and led the way across the street to his house.

As he ushered her into the hall Matilda said, 'I'll only stay for a minute. I should get home and I'm sure you have things to do...'

He didn't answer and Mrs Inch came into the hall then.

'Bless me, miss, you're a sight for sore eyes, to be sure, and it's a pleasure to see you looking so well.' And when Kitty followed her the pair of them hovered over her, beaming.

Presently the doctor said, 'Could we have lunch earlier than usual, Mrs Inch? Miss Paige has to get back to her home.'

'Give me ten minutes,' declared Mrs Inch. 'Let Kitty take your coat and hat, miss, and you and the doctor can have a cosy chat until I'm ready.'

Mrs Inch bustled off and Matilda gave her things to the waiting Kitty. It was only when they were in the drawing room, sitting by the fire with Sam between them, that she said quietly, 'I would rather not have stayed. If I had known...'

Sitting in his chair, completely at ease, he smiled at her.

'We have been working together for some weeks now, haven't we? Isn't it time we got to know each other a little?'

'Why?' asked Matilda.

'I think that we might like each other better if we made the effort.'

Which wasn't the answer she had expected and one which she found difficult to reply to. What would he say, she reflected, if she were to tell him that she loved him, had fallen in love with him right from the start? Probably give her the sack, she thought ruefully.

'Why are you smiling?' he wanted to know.

She shook her head. 'I'm glad the flu epidemic is over. It was all a bit of a rush, wasn't it? Have all your patients recovered?'

He accepted the change in conversation without comment.

'Yes, I'm glad to say. You'll find the surgery pretty busy, though. I take it you will come in on Monday morning?'

'Yes, of course. It will be very nice to see everyone again.'

'You enjoyed your stay with Aunt Kate?'

Her smile was enchanting. 'Oh, yes. It was a most wonderful week. She is so kind, and so is Mrs Chubb. They spoilt me dreadfully.'

A little spoiling wouldn't hurt, thought the doctor. He felt concern for her for it seemed that life at home wasn't all it should be. A pretty woman, he thought, with a plain daughter and taking out her disappointment about that on the girl.

He took his phone from his pocket. 'I'll tell your mother you will be home shortly,' he said. She heard the kindness in his voice and winced at it. His pity was the last thing she wanted; it was a pity that he had been there when she'd got home. She hoped that her mother would be nice on the phone, but it was difficult to tell for he spoke briefly and watching his face gave her no clue.

They had lunch presently: chicken soup not out of a tin; a vast ham on the bone which the doctor carved with a practised skill; a winter salad followed by a mincemeat tart and cream and then coffee.

Matilda enjoyed it all for she was hungry and saw no reason to pretend that she wasn't. And the good food and the glass of wine he poured for her loosened her tongue so that she forgot to be shy and stiff.

The doctor, watching her and listening to her quiet voice, felt a vague stirring of something he had never felt before. He told himself that it was pity and knew that to be wrong. Matilda wasn't to be pitied, nor would she ever accept it.

CHAPTER SIX

MATILDA was driven home by the doctor, but he didn't stop this time. Which was a good thing for her mother was waiting for her, brimming over with ill temper. She held it in check while the doctor carried the groceries into the kitchen, thanking him with a charming smile which turned to thin-lipped annoyance the moment he had gone.

'You should have come straight back here, Matilda. How can you be so selfish, knowing that your father and I were depending on you to bring the groceries?'

'Dr Lovell did say that he was taking me to see Mrs Inch and Kitty, Mother. Haven't you been to Mrs Simpkins' while I've been away?'

'I phoned—a boy brought my order. You didn't expect me to go into the village with all this flu about? I told her I would settle the bills later.'

Matilda started to unpack the bags. 'Mother, Father gives you housekeeping money; what has happened to it?'

Mrs Paige rounded on her. 'Don't you dare to criticise me, Matilda. There are three mouths to feed on a pittance.'

'But, Mother, I pay my share so it's two mouths, isn't it? And we both know that there isn't a lot of money but there is enough if we're careful.'

'Am I not to be considered? Living in this dull little place with no friends and nothing to do, nowhere to go...'

'Well, you go to play bridge with Mrs Milton and her friends, Mother, and she did invite you to help out with the church flowers and the Christmas bazaar. You'll meet lots of people if only you would go to the village sometimes—not just the people you meet at bridge.'

'I shall go and lie down,' declared Mrs Paige. 'You've given me a headache; I quite wish you hadn't come home.'

Matilda put away the food and went to see her father. He looked up from his writing, pleased to see her.

'It is very pleasant to have you home again, my dear. Your mother will be so relieved. She has had so much to do; I only wish that I could do more for her. She deserves a holiday; I must see if I can manage to send her to stay with one of her friends for a few days. She misses them so much.'

He sighed. 'She still thinks of the vicarage as home…'

'Well, perhaps we could manage it between us, Father; it would only be the train fare and the bus to Taunton.'

'She would need money in her purse; I couldn't send her away empty-handed.'

He shuffled the papers on his desk. 'There is a bill which I must pay then perhaps she could go in a week or so.' He said worriedly, 'I don't know where the money goes, my dear. I must be a bad manager.'

'No, you're not, Father; it's just taking time to adjust to living on your pension.'

He had found the bill and she took it from him and said cheerfully, 'Well, we could see to this; are there any more?'

He sifted through the muddle. There were. Her

mother had made no bones about owing the milkman, the newsagent's , the butcher who came twice a week to the village. She had phoned the orders and now, after a month, the bills were coming in. They didn't add up to a great deal but Matilda thought unhappily that they could have been paid with the money she had spent on her coat and dress. Common sense told her that she had no need to feel guilty, but she did.

'If you will see to these, Father,' said Matilda, 'there will be enough money for Mother to go away for a few days.' And when he looked doubtful she said, 'I don't need next week's pay packet…'

Christmas was coming, she reflected; there would be presents to buy, cards to send, extra food. Perhaps if her mother had a few days away she would settle down.

Although the flu epidemic was over, the waiting room was quickly filled on Monday morning: nasty coughs, bad chests, earache—all the minor ailments which made life harder than it needed to be. But everyone was glad to see Matilda, glad to see her well again, anxious to know if she felt really better.

Not quite everyone, though. The doctor, arriving punctually, wished her a cool good morning and made no mention of her health. She was back on her feet again and that was that. And when the last patient had gone he put his head round the door to tell her that he was going to Taunton.

'The answering machine's on and I should be back by early afternoon. Mrs Inch will bring you coffee. Lock up, if you will.'

At least he hadn't called her Miss Paige—he hadn't called her anything.

Mrs Inch had a cup of coffee with her.

'Rushing off like that,' she grumbled, and offered Matilda a biscuit. 'Swallowing his coffee in the kitchen in such a rush. Give himself an ulcer he will. He had a phone call from that Miss Armstrong quite early this morning. I dare say he's going to see her on his way to Taunton.'

Matilda said, 'Quite likely, I dare say. She lives at North Curry, doesn't she? and that's only a mile or two away from Taunton.'

He would be there by now, she thought, and shut her mind to the thought. Being in love with someone was most unsatisfactory when they didn't care a row of pins for you. Possibly one got used to that just as one got used to the small nagging pain of a corn. Not that she knew what that was like; she had pretty feet which gave her no trouble at all...

She called at Mrs Simpkins' for some eggs, listened to that lady's vivid description of her varicose veins with patient sympathy and then went home.

Her mother greeted her coldly; she wasn't to be allowed to feel that she was forgiven, but her father, already busy at his desk, was delighted to see her.

'I have been thinking of our little talk, my dear, and I think your suggestion concerning a little holiday for your mother is most acceptable. Needless to say, I am deeply grateful for your help. I promise you that once we have got our financial situation settled you will be repaid tenfold.'

'Don't worry about that, Father. Mother will be pleased—you must tell her.' She looked at her father; he looked tired and pale. 'You feel all right?'

'Splendid, my dear. I shall talk to your mother presently. I've no doubt that she will lose no time in writing to one of our friends.'

Mrs Paige was mollified by the prospect of a visit with old friends. She grumbled too; she would need money to spend while she was there, she pointed out, and there were bound to be small expenses...

Matilda handed over almost all of her pay packet at the end of the week and hoped it would be enough, although she doubted that. But the visit was to be a short one—five or six days—and if her mother was careful...

So Mrs Paige packed the elegant clothes she had had little opportunity of wearing at Much Winterlow and was put on the bus to Taunton on Saturday afternoon. She would have liked a taxi but, as Matilda explained, there really wasn't enough money for that and since her mother was to be met at Taunton by her friend the journey would be an easy one for her.

Mrs Milton came to drive her father to church on Sunday and Matilda went too, in the new hat and coat, and of course she was thankful that she was wearing them when she saw Lucilla sitting beside the doctor. They were sitting on the other side of the aisle to Mrs Milton and she was careful not to look across to their pew.

After the service she would have slipped out of the church but her father wouldn't be hurried. Even though he didn't go to the village he had friends there—older men who came to see him from time to time—and what better time to exchange a few words than after morning church? Mrs Milton was never in a hurry; they dawdled towards the church door and found the Reverend Mr Milton talking to the doctor. Lucilla was there too, looking bored, and Matilda said quickly to Mrs Milton, 'I'll walk home and have lunch ready for Father. You don't mind? He does so enjoy his weekly chat.'

Which meant that she needed only to bid a general good morning as she passed them. Out of the corner of her eye she saw Lucilla's nasty little smile.

She was up early on Monday morning. It was too soon for her father to get up but she took him a cup of tea and left his breakfast ready for him. 'I'll be back soon after ten o'clock,' she assured him. 'If it's not too cold we could go for a short walk before lunch. You won't be too lonely?'

He was looking tired again, she thought, although he assured her that he had had a good night's sleep.

It was a fine morning, still dark and frosty, and once in the waiting room, not yet warmed by the radiators, she thought longingly of Aunt Kate's cosy cottage. 'Which won't do at all,' said Matilda, addressing the empty room. 'You're back here now, Miss Paige.'

The waiting room filled up rapidly—mostly mothers with small snuffling children who were peevish with colds and coughs. Mrs Trim was there with what she described as a nasty chest and old Mr Trimble was short-tempered by reason of his persistent cough. There was a good deal of talk; Christmas was the main topic: the carol singers and Mrs Simpkins' splendid display of Christmas goods, the play the amateur theatrical society would be putting on, the schoolchildren's concert.

They fell silent when the doctor put his head round the door with a general good morning and the first patient went into the surgery. The hubbub started up again immediately until he returned, often enough to give a highly coloured version of what was wrong with him and give a good deal of good-natured advice to the following patient.

Matilda, sitting in her corner, in her sober dress, sometimes felt like a schoolteacher with an unruly class. But it was all so good-natured and she quite understood that for people living some distance from the village it was a splendid chance to have a good gossip.

The last patient seen, the doctor opened the surgery door.

'Have your coffee before you go, Miss Paige,' he said and went back to sit at his desk, spectacles perched on his handsome nose, a pile of forms before him. He didn't look up as she sat down on the other side of the desk and poured the coffee. He nodded his thanks when she put his cup down at his elbow, and without looking up said, 'Just let me finish these…'

Just as though I was making a nuisance of myself, thought Matilda indignantly, but then he looked up and smiled.

'Would you come with me to Duckett's Farm? I've bad news for Mr Duckett and his wife. There's a small child; I thought that you might come in handy—playing with him and so on so that I can talk to them quietly. Tell me if it's not possible; perhaps you had already arranged to go home. You might like to phone your mother…'

'Mother is staying with friends, Father's alone. If I could let him know that I might be a little late for lunch, of course I'll come. Now?'

'Please. The phone's in the hall if you would like to use it.' He looked at her over his specs and smiled again and her heart turned over.

Duckett's Farm was three miles from the village, rather isolated, with ploughed fields surrounding it and a muddy track leading to the farmyard from a narrow country lane. The house was a fair size but, on this winter day, bleak, huddled in a circle of farm buildings. Matilda wondered if anyone living there could be happy and, as the doctor pushed open the door and she went past him into a warm, low-ceilinged hall, saw that they could. Another door gave her a glimpse of a large room, a roaring fire in the hearth, bright curtains at the small windows. Whoever lived here, she reflected, had made a home.

A voice answered the doctor's hello. 'In the kitchen; I'm just coming.'

A young woman pushed open another door and came towards them, smiling. A small boy toddled beside her and went straight to the doctor, who picked him up and tucked him under an arm.

'Is Rob around, Mrs Duckett?'

She said quickly, 'You've got the results of those tests, Doctor?' When he nodded she said, 'He's in the barn; I'll give him a shout—or do you want to see him alone?'

'I think we must have a talk, Mrs Duckett.' His voice was very kind. 'I've brought my receptionist with me—Matilda Paige; I thought that she might keep an eye on Tom while we go somewhere quiet.'

Mrs Duckett nodded, not trusting herself to speak. But she smiled at Matilda as she went to the door and shouted for her husband. The doctor handed over small Tom to Matilda and he went willingly enough, pleased to see a new face. She hoisted him up and carried him over to a chair by the fire and sat down, talking in her quiet voice, a gentle trickle of sound which took his attention so that he hardly noticed when the doctor told her that they would be back presently and the three of them left the room.

He had told her something of Rob Duckett, a young man still, ignoring a cough and malaise, putting off seeing the doctor until he could no longer ignore the fact that something was wrong. He had been sent for tests and X-rays and the results were what the doctor had expected. And he had the task of telling Rob, knowing that although an operation might be successful Rob might refuse, for who could run the farm while he was away?

Matilda, reciting nursery rhymes, hoped that there would be a solution. The look on Mrs Duckett's face had wrung her heart. She began on 'A Frog he would a-wooing go' and reminded herself that if there was a solution the doctor would find it.

Little Tom liked hearing about the frog, so she recited it again and then again. They came back into the room then but she stayed where she was and since the little boy was quiet on her lap she began on the frog rhyme once more.

Presently Mrs Duckett came across the room to her. She had been crying but her voice was quite steady.

'It's kind of you, miss; he's quite taken to you.'

'He's a darling, isn't he? And do please call me Matilda. Would you like me to do anything for you? Make some tea?'

'I've put the kettle on if you'd like to come into the kitchen?'

Matilda, still cuddling Tom, went with her into the nice old-fashioned kitchen with its scrubbed table and elderly Aga. There was a cat with kittens in a basket and a sheepdog snoozing.

'Do you know,' asked Mrs Duckett, 'about my Rob?'

'Dr Lovell told me a little. I'm so sorry, Mrs Duckett, but Dr Lovell will know what's best to be done and Mr Duckett is young and strong.'

Mrs Duckett put tea in a vast pot. 'He wants Rob to

have an operation; says it's got a good chance of being successful. But Rob isn't wanting that. He's worried about the farm.'

'You want him to have the operation?'

'Me? Yes, of course. But finding someone to come here and help on the farm, just before Christmas, too…'

'But if your husband has the operation soon he might be home by Christmas. He couldn't do anything much, but he'd be here to see to everything, wouldn't he?'

Mrs Duckett was pouring tea into four mugs. 'He's a good man, our doctor.'

'Yes,' said Matilda, 'and I think you could trust him to the ends of the earth.' Something in her voice made her companion look at her sharply.

Driving back presently, Matilda asked, 'What has Mr Duckett decided? It's a terrible thing to happen and he's a young man.'

'He's agreed to an operation and since he is a young man he has an excellent chance of recovery.'

'Good. But he was worried about the farm.'

'I think that can be sorted out.'

Not exactly a snub but she had the strong feeling that he thought she was being nosy. But even if he did he was going to make use of her.

'I shall drive him to hospital the day after tomorrow. Mrs Duckett will go with us. I would be glad if you would stay at the farm with Tom. I shall be bringing back her mother who will look after the place while he is away.'

'Alone? Me, I mean, with Tom.'

'John who helps with the milking will be there. You're not a nervous girl, are you?'

'No,' said Matilda in a voice positive enough to convince herself as well as him.

'Good. I'll drive you home.'

She hadn't expected him to get out of the car when they reached the cottage, but he did, following her into the hall just as though she had invited him.

She said pointedly, 'Do come in, Doctor.'

'Well, I am in, aren't I? I'd like to take a look at your father.'

The reasonable remark made her feel a fool. She offered coffee and when he accepted flounced off to the kitchen, her face red.

She took the coffee to her father's study when it was ready and the doctor took the tray from her with the air of a man who expected her to go away again at once.

It was high time to prepare their lunch. She had laid the table, and the soup was on the stove and eggs beaten for an omelette when he came into the kitchen. He had the coffee tray with him and set it tidily by the sink.

'When will your mother be back?' he asked.

'Well, she was coming back on Thursday but she phoned yesterday evening to say that she might stay a day or two longer. Is Father all right? Should she come back? I mean, he has to spend a good part of the day alone.'

'There's nothing to worry about at the moment and there is no reason why he shouldn't be alone for a few hours at a time. But if you will allow me to do so I'll get Kitty or Mrs Inch to come here on Wednesday while you are at Duckett's Farm. Your father has no objection and they can see to lunch and give him tea before they go. I should be back by five o'clock at the latest. I'm sorry I didn't think of this earlier but little Tom likes you and they live in too isolated a place for anyone to be prepared to go there at short notice.' And at her look he added, 'I regard you as a sensible young woman able to cope.'

Should she tell him that she was terrified of meeting a bull, or a large herd of cows, for that matter, and that the idea of spending the day miles from anywhere with a small boy and an unknown farm-hand really didn't appeal?

She looked up at his calm face and decided to say nothing. With her loving him so much it was a foregone conclusion that she would, if necessary, go through fire and water for him, so why boggle at a bull or two?

She said sedately, 'You have arranged things very well, Doctor. It will be nice for Father to have company.' She remembered something then. 'You said that there was nothing to worry about for the moment. Will you explain that?'

'Your father is well; I examined him thoroughly. I have no wish to alarm you but you should know that someone with his heart condition could be taken ill at any time, probably without warning. You are sensible enough to realise that there is no point in anticipating something which may never happen. All the same you should know, and I think your mother should understand that too.'

He studied her quiet face, smiled and went to the door. She went with him and he paused as he reached it and bent and kissed her. A gentle kiss and somehow reassuring.

She watched him get into the car and drive away and then went back into the kitchen and got out the frying-pan, wondering about the kiss. He would have no idea what it had done to her, of course; probably he had bestowed it with the same kindly intent with which he would have stroked a kitten or indeed comforted a crying child. But it mustn't happen again.

He was his usual remote self at the evening surgery; beyond wishing her goodnight when it was finished, he had nothing to say.

She got her father's breakfast ready before she left on Wednesday morning, reassured by his obvious pleasure at the prospect of company for lunch. He told her to go and enjoy herself. She hoped she would but she was doubtful about it.

There was a mercifully short surgery; they drank their coffee in silence while the doctor wrote then went out to the car. It was a cold, blustery day and she shivered as they got out of the car at the farm.

There were lights on in the downstairs rooms and Mr and Mrs Duckett were waiting in the kitchen. There was a youngish man there too—John, who grinned and ducked his head at them.

'There's been no time,' began Mrs Duckett rather wildly. 'There's soup ready and a milk pudding in the oven. You'll manage?'

'Don't worry, Mrs Duckett, we'll be fine. And good luck, Mr Duckett.' And, because Mrs Duckett looked so forlorn, Matilda kissed her cheek and picked up little Tom so that he could say goodbye.

They didn't waste time. 'See you around five o'clock,' said the doctor, and drove his passengers away without a backward glance.

Beyond a faint whimper, Tom didn't cry. Matilda

sat him in his high chair, offered him a rusk and turned to John.

'You won't be far away?' she asked.

'Got to turn the cows out into the lower field, then I muck out the barn, come in for a mug of tea and then see to the feed. I'll be around if you need me, miss. I'll be off now—a bit behind already.'

By five o'clock Matilda was tired. She'd been busy finding her way around the house, peering into cupboards, hunting for the tea, sugar, salt—all the day-to-day things which were never where she expected them to be, as well as feeding Tom and John, the dog and a family of cats. She'd played with Tom, and while he had a nap after their midday meal she'd ironed the pile of washing which she was sure Mrs Duckett wouldn't feel like doing.

John had been a great help, but he had his work to do: the milking and the feeding, the small flock of sheep to check, coming indoors from time to time for a mug of tea.

'Good thing the missus 'as got 'er ma coming back with 'er—lives at 'Atch Beauchamp. She'll stay a while until things are sorted.'

'And you'll be here to run the farm, John?'

'Yup.'

'Shouldn't you be going home about now?'

'Yup—but I'll stay till the doctor comes. 'E said five o'clock and 'e's a man of 'is word.'

Matilda, sitting at the kitchen table and coaxing a sleepy Tom to eat his supper, hoped that he was right.

And he was. She saw the car's headlights as it entered the yard and a moment later Mrs Duckett and an older woman came in, followed by the doctor.

He nodded at Matilda, greeted John and said cheerfully, 'Sorry we are a bit late. Everything all right?'

John said, 'Yup,' and Matilda nodded. Mrs Duckett had gone at once to Tom and her mother was taking off her coat and hat.

'The kettle is boiling,' said Matilda. 'Shall I make tea?'

'You'll want to go on home, miss,' said Mrs Duckett. 'I'm grateful. Has Tom been good?'

'As gold. We've had a lovely day together and John's been a marvellous help.'

She wanted to ask about Mr Duckett but hesitated. Supposing it was bad news? But Mrs Duckett forestalled her. 'Rob's having his operation in the morning. Doctor's fixed someone to take me to the hospital in the afternoon and I can stay if I need to now Mother's here.'

She managed a smile. 'He says everything will be all right…'

'And it will be,' said Matilda, 'if he said so.'

The doctor, talking to John, heard that and allowed himself a little smile.

He drove her home then, stopping briefly at his own home on the way. And at the cottage he went in with her, spent a few moments with her father, thanked her briefly and went away again, and this time he didn't kiss her.

Her father had had a pleasant day. Mrs Inch had come at lunchtime and cooked a delicious meal and stayed for an early cup of tea.

'And she told me to tell you that she had left our supper on the stove.'

And when Matilda went to look there was a casserole only needing to be heated up. It looked delicious and her mouth watered.

The week resumed its normal sober pattern. The waiting room filled and emptied, the doctor bade her good morning and good evening, took himself off to Taunton and his far-flung patients, and although he invited her to share his coffee in the mornings she found some excuse not to accept. He showed no sign of minding this but he did keep her informed about Rob Duckett. The operation had been successful; he was still in Intensive Care and would be in hospital for some time yet, but there was a good chance that he would be home for Christmas.

The doctor gave her this information in a business-like way, told her that he had been out to the farm and that Mrs Duckett and Tom sent their love. 'Tom's a nice child...'

'He's a darling,' said Matilda warmly.

'You like children?'

'Yes,' said Matilda. Especially if they were her own and the doctor was their father. Only she didn't say that.

She was glad when it was Friday and she had some money. Her mother had phoned again; friends of the friends she was staying with intended to drive to their daughter's home at Wellington and had offered her a lift, on Sunday.

'It's not too far out of their way,' she had explained. 'I've asked them to stay for tea. We should be home about three o'clock, so have tea ready for four o'clock, Matilda. Get scones and make a cake and see that there's a good fire in the sitting room. Don't fetch your father to the phone; we're just going out to dinner and there's no time. Give him my love.'

So Matilda walked down to Mrs Simpkins' on
Saturday morning and presently emerged with two
plastic bags and a lighter purse. The doctor, standing
at his window, watched her going off home, frowning.
It was no concern of his, of course, but Matilda didn't
appear to have much fun in her life. No sign of a boyfriend, drab clothes except for the new coat and hat.
He might suggest that she might like a few days' holiday before Christmas. Aunt Kate would be delighted
to have her again. He might even go over and take her
out—dinner perhaps?

He turned away to answer the telephone. It was
Lucilla, inviting him in a coaxing voice to take her out
to lunch. And since it was his day off he agreed. But
later, sitting opposite her at the Castle Hotel in
Taunton, he found himself wishing that it were Matilda
sitting there and not Lucilla.

Mr Paige, warmly wrapped up, was fetched to church
on Sunday morning by Mrs Milton, leaving Matilda
free to get lunch and do some baking. While the cake
was in the oven she hoovered and dusted, arranged the
very last of the chrysanthemums in a vase, and lit the
fire in the sitting room. She got out the best china too,
and the silver teaspoons, and put everything out ready
for tea. Rastus, watching her from his chair in the
kitchen, yawned and went to sleep, but, having no one
else to talk to, Matilda went on talking to him.

'It will be nice to see Mother again,' she told him,
'and I dare say that now she's had a holiday she will
feel much more settled. And there's Christmas to look
forward to.'

Mrs Milton had mentioned several social events in
the village; perhaps they could all go. Her father, once

he could be prised from his books and writing, enjoyed meeting people...

Her mother arrived home soon after three o'clock and two people came with her—a large red-faced man, middle-aged and with a loud voice, and a very thin woman of about the same age, most elegantly dressed and with a voice almost as loud as her husband's. Mrs Paige, wearing a new hat, Matilda saw with a sinking heart, ushered her guests in with little cries of apology.

'Come in, come in. Our funny little cottage—only temporary of course. And this is our daughter, Matilda.'

She didn't wait for Matilda to do more than shake hands. 'Fetch your father, Matilda. Take off your coats and come into the sitting room. At least it will be warm there.'

Matilda fetched her father and they went together to the sitting room where Mrs Paige greeted him effusively and then caught Matilda's eye.

'We'll have tea now. I hope it's quite ready.'

Their guests made a splendid tea and, taking a second slice of cake, pronounced it delicious.

'Oh, Matilda cooks quite well. Such a help to me. It seems so strange that someone as delicate as I am should have such a sensible, practical daughter.'

Two pairs of eyes studied Matilda. From their expressions she guessed that they agreed with her mother, dismissing her as plain and uninteresting but handy to have around. Well, thought Matilda, I am, and smiled at them so that for the moment she wasn't plain at all.

They left presently and her mother embarked on an excited account of the visit. 'I felt so well while I was there; I feel I can face life here once more, and I found a marvellous book for you, dear.' She smiled at Mr Paige. 'I hope it's what you will enjoy.

'And I've something for you, Matilda: gloves—woolly gloves. To keep your hands warm when you go out in the mornings.' She added, 'And I have bought one or two things for myself—the shops were so tempting.'

'That's a pretty hat,' said Matilda.

'Isn't it? I felt rather naughty buying it—it was rather more than I usually pay—but I couldn't resist it. I've spent every penny...'

And when Mr Paige looked worried she said, 'Don't worry, dear; I know Matilda will help out until your pension is paid into the bank.'

Matilda wondered just what would happen if she said that she wasn't going to help out. Something she would never do because of her father. A quiet life and no worries, the doctor had said.

She presented her usual quiet face at the surgery on Monday morning, presided over the waiting room with her habitual good nature and, when bidden to drink coffee with the doctor when the surgery was closed, politely refused.

A waste of breath. 'I have something to say to you,' said the doctor in a voice which wasn't going to take no for an answer.

But it wasn't until she had almost drunk her coffee that he spoke.

'I think it might be a good idea if you were to have a few days' holiday.'

'But I've just had one with Miss Lovell. Aren't I being satisfactory?'

'You are perfectly satisfactory, Matilda. And that wasn't a holiday, that was convalescence after flu. You may tell me that it is none of my business if you wish, but it seems to me that you have very little opportunity to enjoy life. Have you no young friends of your own age? Men friends? You should be thinking about marriage, a home of your own. Your mother depends upon you, doesn't she? But she has no need to do so. She is able to run her home and look after your father without your help. Have you ever considered leaving home? You are perfectly capable of earning your own living.'

'You think I should go away from here?' And never see you again? she added silently.

'See something of the world, meet people, travel, perhaps?'

He found himself disliking that idea even as he uttered it. It was all very well suggesting that she should go and make a life for herself, but only if there was someone with her to look after her. She might be sensible and practical but she knew nothing of the world.

'Anyway, take a few days off before Christmas. Go shopping and pay Aunt Kate a visit.'

'I'll have to talk it over with Mother and Father—they may have planned something.'

'Just as you wish. I may be a little late this evening. Will you let the patients know?'

He had called her Matilda but now they were back at the beginning again. It was never going to be any different. She went quietly away and he didn't look up from his desk.

CHAPTER SEVEN

MRS PAIGE welcomed Matilda's news that she was to take a brief holiday with unexpected enthusiasm.

'But how fortunate. As you will be home all day for a few days I shall be able to go to Taunton. We must start to think of Christmas; there will be presents to buy and cards—and you will be home to help me write them. Lady Truscott is giving a dinner party; we are sure to be invited. And I really must return the hospitality I have received—a coffee morning, perhaps.'

Matilda didn't say anything. The doctor had mentioned Aunt Kate but she thought that he had done so in order to persuade her to have some days off. She didn't want them but she couldn't tell him that they would be spent at home for the most part.

All that nonsense about men friends... In bed that night she cried about that, making Rastus, curled up beside her, very damp.

On Wednesday morning, when the surgery was over, she asked him when he would like her to have her days off.

He looked at her, as neat as a new pin, sitting opposite him, drinking the coffee he'd insisted that she should have.

She was pale and there were shadows under her eyes. Lovely eyes, he conceded. There was a good deal he would have liked to say but Matilda could be contrary and tart and withdraw into her shell...

He said pleasantly, 'Are you going to the annual dance at the village hall on Saturday?' He didn't give her time to answer. 'Because if you haven't already made arrangements, will you come with me? Everyone goes—and I mean everyone.'

'Me? Go with you?' said Matilda. 'But what about Miss Armstrong?'

'What about Miss Armstrong?' asked the doctor silkily. 'I wasn't aware we were talking about her.'

'Well, of course we weren't, 'said Matilda sharply, 'but ought you not to invite her?' She added, 'She might mind.'

'Lucilla is in the South of France and I hardly think she would have any objection to our more or less obligatory appearance together at a village function.'

'Oh, well,' said Matilda, 'in that case I'll come. Thank you for asking me. What should I wear?'

It would be a pleasure, reflected the doctor, to pop Matilda into his car and take her to a boutique and buy her the prettiest dress there. The thought surprised him so that he didn't answer at once.

'Not black tie,' he assured her, and saw her small sigh of relief. 'The women wear pretty dresses—you know, the kind of thing they wear to weddings and christenings. The dancing is a bit old-fashioned and there's a local band. This is a friendly village—but you have discovered that, haven't you?'

'Yes, it sounds fun.'

'Oh, it is; the vicar gives prizes and there's beer and ham sandwiches.'

She smiled then and a little colour came into her cheeks and he went on, 'I'm having a few days off myself next week. Will that suit you? And Aunt Kate wants you to go and stay, even if it's only for a day or so. She's writing to you.'

'I'd like to see her again but I'm not sure… Mother would like to go to Taunton and if I'm at home she can leave Father all day. And she is going to have a coffee morning.'

'That still leaves three or four days. Aunt Kate declared that she will drive over and fetch you.'

'Oh—I should very much like to see her again. I'll— I'll talk to Mother.'

'Good. I'm going to the Ducketts. Rob is making excellent progress; he should be home for Christmas. Tom wants to see you again.'

'Does he? I'll borrow Mrs Simpkins' bike and go one afternoon. Mrs Duckett wouldn't mind?'

'Mrs Duckett happens to think you are a very nice young lady.' He got up to go. 'As indeed you are, Matilda.'

Matilda, pink in the face, wished him a muttered good morning and whisked herself back into the waiting room.

The postman drove up just as she reached the cottage. There was a letter for her from Aunt Kate—easily identified by the fine spidery writing and expensive notepaper. Matilda dawdled up the garden path, reading it.

Aunt Kate was inviting her to stay for the last two days of her holiday. She would drive over and fetch her and she would not take no for an answer.

Armed with that, Matilda went indoors to find her mother. Who wasn't pleased. 'How tiresome. It won't do to offend the old lady, I suppose. I shall have to do my shopping at the beginning of the week and have my coffee morning on the Thursday. Really, people are most inconsiderate.'

'And Dr Lovell has asked me to go to the annual dance at the village hall.'

'Asked *you*? Whatever for? He's more or less engaged to that Armstrong girl.'

'She's in France...'

'Oh, well, I suppose he has to show up at those village functions and take someone with him. Farm labourers, I suppose...'

It was hard to like her mother sometimes. 'Yes, I expect so,' said Matilda.

If the doctor was looking forward to their Saturday outing he gave no sign of it. The patients waiting their turn at the surgery were full of it. Everyone was going, it seemed. It was an event not to be missed. Matilda, asked countless times if she was going, said yes, she was, but she didn't say who with. The doctor might have invited her but anything could happen before Saturday...

It wasn't until Friday evening, as she was clearing up after the last patient had left, that he opened the waiting-room door to speak to her about it.

'I'll call for you about half past seven,' he told her. 'It starts at seven o'clock and everyone makes a point of getting there as early as possible.' He stood looking at her. 'You're going to Aunt Kate's at the end of next week?'

'Yes, Friday and Saturday. I'm looking forward to that.'

He nodded. 'Good. I shall be away most of the week myself. Dr Ross will come over each day and bring his nurse with him. He'll be on call for emergencies. I hope everyone read the notice in the waiting room?'

'Yes, they did, and I told Mrs Simpkins.'

'Ah, yes. A wise move. Goodnight, Miss Paige.'

Miss Paige again, thought Matilda. He would be going to the South of France to be with Lucilla, of course. They would go together to the dance and he would dance the first dance with her and then hand her over politely to whoever was nearest.

'For two pins I won't go,' said Matilda, knowing that nothing on earth would stop her.

She was ready long before half past seven on Saturday; she had been afraid that some last-minute thing would hinder her and now she was in the sitting room with her mother and father. She had spent a long time on her hair and face but the result was exactly as usual. Only the new dress was a success. Even her mother had admired it, adding that it was a pity that Matilda couldn't do anything about her hair. 'You need to go to a good hairdresser and have a good cut and highlights.' But she hadn't said any more in case Matilda took her advice and spent money on the hairdresser Mrs Paige intended to visit if she could wheedle some money out of Matilda's purse...

Mr Paige said mildly, 'You look very pretty, my dear. I dare say you will have a delightful evening. I expect you will know many of the people there.'

Mrs Paige said impatiently, 'It is a village dance, dear; no one I know will be there. I suppose Dr Lovell feels that he must make an appearance.'

Matilda put on her coat; she had heard the squeak of the garden gate and a moment later came a knock on the door. She went to let the doctor in and he spent a moment or so with her father and mother before saying briskly, 'Shall we go? Have you a key? I don't suppose we shall be back before midnight.'

'Oh, I'll stay up,' said Mrs Paige. 'I usually keep early hours but I can always have a doze during the day. I do get so tired...'

'In that case there is no need for you to stay up, Mrs Paige. I'm sure Matilda is old enough to have a key.'

'Certainly she is,' said Mr Paige. 'Let her have yours, my dear.'

Matilda kissed him goodnight, received the key from her mother, who turned her cheek away, and went out to the car with the doctor. She wished that she could think of something light-hearted to say but her mother had cast a blight over the evening; she hadn't said much but somehow she had managed to cast a damper...

However, it seemed that the doctor hadn't noticed; he talked cheerfully about nothing much until they reached the village hall where he parked the car and ushered her inside. It was crowded and so noisy that the band could scarcely be heard. It was quite a large hall and it had been decorated with balloons and old-fashioned paper chains and it was evident that everyone was having a good time.

Matilda took off her coat and added it to the pile inside the door, then the doctor took her arm and swung her onto the dance floor.

'I like the dress,' he said to the top of her head. He sounded as though he meant it, too.

He danced well, she discovered, and although she hadn't had much opportunity to go dancing she was a good dancer. He would see friends—people she didn't know—and dance with them presently, she supposed, but just for the moment she was happy.

The crush was terrific and after a minute or two she began to pick out people she knew: Mrs Simpkins in red velvet dancing with a small man, presumably her husband; the pub owner, who shouted greetings to her; several patients, not easily recognised in their best clothes; the Reverend Mr and Mrs Milton; Lady Truscott and several of the ladies her mother had introduced her to from the bridge circle. And they were all enjoying themselves...

Presently the band leader announced an excuse-me dance and she was swept away from the doctor's arms into the jovial embrace of the milkman and then to a succession of partners—Mr Milton, the postman, the pub owner, and then, thankfully, the doctor once more.

'Enjoying yourself?' he wanted to know, and when the band stopped playing he found a quiet corner for her and then fetched ham sandwiches and a fizzy drink for her and beer for himself.

They danced again and Matilda, in his arms, had never been so happy. And the doctor, his arm encircling her small person, knew a deep contentment, as though he had found something he had been looking for and had found unexpectedly.

It was almost midnight when Lady Truscott, standing breathless beside them after a rousing quick-step, suggested that they should go back to her place for hot drinks. 'I'll collect the rest of us,' she told them. She smiled at Matilda. 'It's the done thing,' she confided. 'We slip away about now, and so do some of the older ones here, so that the younger ones can finish the evening with a disco.'

Before Matilda could say anything the doctor said, 'We would like that,' and then, to her, 'Don't worry; I'll take you home whenever you want to go.'

Lady Truscott's house was ablaze with lights and her housekeeper was waiting with hot coffee, tiny sausage rolls and hot mince pies. Matilda, looking round her, saw that as well as her own friends Lady Truscott had gathered several people from the village—Mrs Simpkins and her husband, several of the farmers and their wives from the local farms, the Reverend Mr and Mrs Milton, the peppery old colonel who lived opposite the church, and the pub owner and milkman. It was going to be difficult to explain to her mother.

She found herself standing beside the colonel, who, once you got to know him, wasn't peppery at all but talked about his garden, and when she told him what she planned to do with the cottage garden he promised her some seedlings in the spring. They were joined presently by Mr Simpkins, who, it appeared, was as keen a gardener as the colonel, and the doctor, watching from the other side of the room, saw Matilda's absorbed face, alight with interest.

How was it that he had considered her plain? She was nothing of the sort; her face was one at which it was a delight to look. He listened with apparent attention to Lady Truscott's descriptions of the various delights in store at the Christmas bazaar, assured her that he would be there, and added, 'This has been a delightful evening, Mary; you always organise things so well...'

Lady Truscott laughed. 'What else can an elderly widow do with her days, Henry? Do you have to go so soon?'

'I'm taking Matilda home.'

'What a dear creature she is, and so pretty in that dress. A pity she doesn't get out more but her mother assures me that she is a homebird and doesn't care for much social life.'

A remark which he very much doubted.

He went across the room to Matilda and gently prised her away from the milkman and the colonel, watched her as she bade them goodbye and thanked her hostess with pretty manners, found her coat for her and stuffed her into the car.

'What a lovely evening,' declared Matilda. 'I wish it could have gone on for ever!' She glanced sideways at the doctor's calm profile. 'Thank you for inviting me; parties like that make it seem like Christmas, don't you think?'

She chatted on happily. 'Lady Truscott is such a friendly person and I thought the sandwiches at the party were delicious. I'm not sure what I had to drink; it tasted a bit like strong lemonade.'

'A special drink which I believe the committee agreed upon,' said the doctor gravely, knowing it was hardly lemonade and certainly potent enough—despite Lady Truscott's excellent coffee—to loosen Matilda's normally prudent tongue.

'I'm quite sleepy,' volunteered Matilda, and then added, 'We're on holiday next week...'

'Indeed we are.'

'Are you going away?'

'For two or three days.'

He had stopped by the cottage gate and leaned across to undo her safety belt. 'Oh, of course—to the South of France,' said Matilda, and nodded. For a moment the lemonade got the upper hand. 'You're making a mistake!' she told him.

She walked up the garden path with his arm around

her, and waited while he unlocked the door. He pushed her gently inside.

She looked up at him with sleepy eyes. 'I'll never forget,' she told him. He didn't answer, only smiled down at her and closed the door quite quietly.

She had been right, of course, he reflected as he got into the car and sat waiting until he saw a light go on in an upstairs room. He had made a mistake.

In the cold light of early Sunday morning Matilda tried to remember just what she had said to the doctor. She suspected that she had spoken with an unguarded tongue but her recollection was a little vague. He hadn't said much, though, so she couldn't have allowed her tongue to run away with her.

Her mother asked if she had enjoyed herself.

'Very much. The hall was packed and there was a good band. And just before midnight we went to Lady Truscott's and had coffee and sausage rolls and mince pies.'

'Lady Truscott's? Who else was there?'

'Mrs Simpkins and her husband, and the milkman and that nice old colonel—and most of the ladies with whom you play bridge. Oh, and the pub owner and his wife.'

'Not at Lady Truscott's, surely?' Mrs Paige sounded horrified.

'Oh, yes. She was at the dance; so were Mr and Mrs Milton—and that nice man who runs the bank on the opening days.'

'The doctor brought you home?'

'Yes, mother.'

'If I had known,' said Mrs Paige, 'I could have gone to this dance; I didn't realise that it was for everyone.

I could have got someone to come and give your father an hour or two's company, or I could have gone with Dr Lovell…'

'But it was me he invited,' said Matilda mildly.

'Only because Lucilla Armstrong is away, so I hear. He had to take someone, I suppose.' She added crossly, 'I'm not going to church; I've one of my sick headaches coming on. If anyone enquires about me you can say that I haven't been very well for the past few days.'

So Matilda went to church with her father and, beyond a few brief remarks at her mother's absence, no one showed much interest. The congregation, considering how late most of them had been up the night before, was large, and beyond a quick good morning she had no need to say anything to the doctor. However, she couldn't help hearing him tell the vicar that he was leaving directly after lunch, and she heard the vicar urging him to drive carefully—'For you are going quite a distance, Henry.'

All the way to the South of France, reflected Matilda.

She thought about him for the rest of Sunday and all of Monday—a day given over to the washing and ironing and rummaging in cupboards in search of the best china and the silver coffee spoons while her mother sat at the kitchen table planning her coffee morning.

'Wouldn't coffee and biscuits do?' asked Matilda.

'Certainly not. There had better be hot chocolate and some of those herb teas. No biscuits—petit fours and tiny sausage rolls and mince pies and those almond biscuits. And you needn't look like that,' said Mrs Paige sharply. 'Your father has given me the house-keeping money. The money you pay me each week will tide us over…'

'Until when?' asked Matilda.

'Well, your next week's wages, of course. Really, Matilda, you are most ungrateful. I am going to a great deal of trouble to entertain the right people.'

Her mother went to Taunton the next day, grumbling because she had to go by bus, and Matilda took the opportunity to tidy her father's desk and make sure that there weren't any bills tucked in among his books and papers. And since it was a fairly mild day the pair of them took a short walk, talking about the garden and what Matilda hoped to do in the spring.

They ate their lunch in the kitchen because it was the warmest room in the house, and Matilda conjured up an economical supper before she lighted the fire in the sitting room. They sat round it eating buttered toast and doing the *Telegraph* crossword puzzle, very content in each other's company.

Mrs Paige was to return on the afternoon bus, but since by the time it reached Much Winterlow it was dark Matilda walked down to the village to meet her and carry the parcels.

Mrs Paige had had a splendid day having her hair done and shopping, but she was quick to point out that returning on the bus had quite spoilt the day. 'So crowded,' she complained, 'and I had so many parcels. I must talk to your father and persuade him that we must have a car.'

'There isn't enough money, Mother,' said Matilda bleakly. 'Besides, you don't need to go to Taunton every day.'

'If I had a car I could get away from this dull place.'

'Mother, if only you would try and like it—there's so much to do in the village and I don't mean bridge parties.'

She was told not to talk rubbish as her mother went past her into the cottage.

Matilda, unpacking bags and boxes under her mother's eye, noted with a sinking heart the expensive vol-au-vents, petit fours, tiny buns filled with cream and salmon mousse tartlets. Far too much for a friendly coffee morning and heaven only knew what they had cost.

'I've tired myself out,' declared her mother. 'You must hoover the sitting room and make sure the house is fit to be seen. You'll have all day tomorrow in which to do it…'

As it happened, Matilda found time to go into the garden too. It was a wild day with a cold wind but she was soon glowing, collecting up the last of the fallen leaves, raking the beds clear of debris. The dark sky and wild, scudding clouds suited her mood. Was she to be condemned for ever to her mother's beck and call? she wondered. The plain answer was yes, because of her father.

Matilda, preparing for the coffee morning, hardly noticed what she was doing. Tomorrow she would be going to Aunt Kate's house and she could hardly wait. And because she was so happy about that she did everything she could to please her mother. And Mrs Paige needed a lot of pleasing; her coffee morning was to be an elegant affair not easily forgotten.

Lady Truscott came; so did Mrs Milton and the various acquaintances Mrs Paige had made at bridge parties she had been to. And if they were surprised at the elaborate spread put before them they didn't say so. They were happy living at Much Winterlow and felt sorry for anyone who wasn't. Of course they realised

that, after the busy life of committees, meetings and
parochial gatherings, Mrs Paige might find village life
dull. Dull from her point of view, of course, not theirs.
There was more than enough to keep life interesting:
Farmer Squire's cow having triplets, Mrs Trim winning
a few hundred pounds in the lottery, the Kentons' el-
dest boy getting a scholarship to Sherborne, and now
Christmas looming...

They drank the excellent coffee and ate the dainties
they were offered, then told their hostess quite sin-
cerely they had enjoyed themselves, at the same time
urging her to join in the village activities.

'I know that you couldn't leave your husband,' said
Lady Truscott kindly, 'but you would have enjoyed the
dance. How beautifully Matilda dances. She and the
doctor made a splendid pair and she never lacked for
partners. She is very popular in the village, you know;
a charming girl.'

When everyone had gone and they were clearing up
Mrs Paige remarked with a little laugh, 'Lady Truscott
said you were charming. A pity Dr Lovell is going to
marry Lucilla Armstrong; you might have stood a
chance with him.'

'Most unlikely, said Matilda cheerfully. 'I work for
him.' Her smile hid the hurtful thought that even with
no competition she had no chance of attracting him.
She would go on working for him too until she retired,
like Miss Brimble, to look after an aged parent.

Then she remembered that she was going to stay
with Aunt Kate and life became once more an adven-
ture, for who knew what lay around the next corner?

Miss Lovell, in sensible tweeds and a severe hat, arrived punctually in the morning. She accepted coffee,

listening to Mrs Paige's account of her coffee morning and enjoying a brief talk with Mr Paige before putting down her cup and saucer and declaring that they must be off.

'I'll bring Matilda back on Sunday evening,' she told them. 'After supper.'

In the car, driving like Jehu through the country roads, Aunt Kate observed, 'You're looking pale, Matilda. Does Henry work you too hard?'

'Heavens, no! I'm only part-time, you know, and I love the work. It's not at all hard.'

'Done any Christmas shopping yet?'

Aunt Kate avoided a farm trailer by a hair's breadth.

'No—well, I bought my Christmas cards from Mrs Simpkins' shop, and wrapping paper and labels. I must go to Taunton and buy presents.'

'Or you can do some shopping in Somerton. The town shops are exciting but I find I can get all I want in the local shops.'

Matilda, her purse moderately filled for once, agreed happily. She hadn't many presents to get and she knew what she wanted to buy. She had worried about the doctor. Should she give him a present? Something impersonal like a diary? She suspected that he got several from the medical firms who were always sending samples. You couldn't give a man flowers unless he was in bed ill; he didn't smoke. A desk calendar, perhaps.

Miss Lovell stopped with a flourish before her door and Mrs Chubb was there, bidding them to come in from the cold, bustling around them, urging Matilda up the stairs to her room with the warning to go straight downstairs again to drink her coffee before it got cold.

'And I can see you're in need of a bit of cosseting.

Been working too hard, I'll be bound. All work and no play...you know what they say!'

'But I went to the annual village dance on Saturday, Mrs Chubb. It was lovely.'

'That's as may be; you could do with a few more pounds on you too.'

Saying which, Mrs Chubb took herself downstairs again.

'She don't look happy, Miss Lovell,' she declared, carrying in the coffee tray. 'Now why is that? In love?'

Aunt Kate picked up the coffee pot. 'I think there is that possibility,' she said thoughtfully. 'We'll know soon enough.'

'If you say so, ma'am.'

A few moments later Matilda uttered a small sigh as she entered the sitting room. There was a splendid fire burning, the coffee smelled delicious and Taffy went to meet her.

'He remembers me,' said Matilda happily. Her small nose wrinkled with pleasure. Life for the moment was everything—well, almost everything—she could wish for.

They lunched presently: one of Mrs Chubb's nourishing soups, a soufflé as light as feathers and a winter salad. And a glass of wine with it.

'And now make your list, child,' said Miss Lovell. 'We will go to Somerton and take a look round the shops.'

There was more than enough choice for Matilda's modest list. A silk scarf for her mother, and after a search around a bookshop just the book her father had mentioned he would like to have. Fine lawn hankies for Mrs Inch and chocolates for Kitty and, after consulta-

tion with Aunt Kate, a bead necklace for Mrs Chubb.
There was still Aunt Kate, of course, and the doctor,
but she was running out of money and their gifts would
need a good deal of thought.

They had tea at an elegant little café—toasted tea-
cakes and a dish of mouth-watering cream cakes and a
large pot of tea. Aunt Kate wasn't a woman to do
things by halves.

It had begun to rain as they left the café and it was
already dark, which made Aunt Kate's sitting room a
haven of comfort and warmth when they reached it
And presently they sat down to supper: steak and kidney pie, its pastry lid a masterpiece of perfection,
Brussels sprouts and potatoes mashed to a creamy
smoothness, and then one of Mrs Chubb's trifles. All
helped down with a glass of claret.

Matilda, curled up in her pretty bed, slept all night.
Her last thoughts were of Dr Lovell, of course, as were
her waking ones too.

The rain disappeared during the night and the next
day it was chilly with a strong wind. But here and there
were patches of pale blue sky.

'Brisk walk,' said Miss Lovell, watching Matilda
spooning her porridge. 'Nothing like it. We'll take the
footpath to Thors Magna and have coffee at the pub
there.'

Which they did—a couple of miles across country
with the promised coffee at the end of it. There was
time for a quick look round the church before they
walked back to another of Mrs Chubb's nourishing
meals.

'I shall take a nap after lunch,' declared Aunt Kate.
'Put on a coat and explore the garden if you would like

to. There are books and magazines in the garden room, so help yourself. Tea at half past four.'

So presently Matilda got into the elderly hooded cloak which Mrs Chubb offered her and went into the garden. She had been there before but now she explored it thoroughly, admiring the brick paths between the flowerbeds, the little summer house right at the end of the garden and the vegetable patch hidden behind a cunningly planted circle of small fruit trees. She would do something like that, she decided. Once winter was over she could spend more time in the garden. And a little summer house would be just the thing for her father. She went and had another look at it, wondering how much it would cost, poking her head inside to get a better look.

Dr Lovell, coming silently across the lawn, stopped to watch her. There wasn't much of her to be seen for the cloak enveloped her entirely and he smiled as he spoke.

'You are in there under the tent thing?' he asked.

Matilda shot up, got entangled in the cloak and had to be set back on her feet. She said the first thing to enter her head and then bitterly regretted it.

'Why aren't you in the South of France?'

'Am I supposed to be there?'

Matilda wrapped the cloak tightly around her. It was a kind of refuge and she felt in need of one. 'Well, no, I just thought that that was where you would be with Lucilla.'

'I had no idea that you were so interested in my private life, Matilda.'

Matilda said coldly, 'You are mistaken; I am not in the least interested.' And that was a waste of breath for he laughed. She turned her back on him then and wished that he would go away although in her heart she knew she would hate it if he did...

'Let us bury the hatchet,' said the doctor mildly. 'Let us ignore our private lives—yours as well as mine—and I for one am prepared to show a true Christmas spirit and invite you to have dinner with me this evening.'

'Dinner? With you? What about Aunt Kate? I mean, she'll come with us?'

He said silkily, 'Afraid to be alone in my company, Matilda?'

'Of course not. What a very silly thing to say. I'd like to have dinner with you if Aunt Kate wouldn't mind.'

'Then let us go indoors and tell her. Mrs Chubb was rattling the teacups when I arrived.'

He put a vast arm around her shoulders and walked her back into the kitchen, where he unwound her from the cloak, waited while she kicked off the wellies she had borrowed, and urged her into the sitting room.

Miss Lovell had had her nap and was knitting. She looked up as they went in. 'You'll be wanting your tea. What do you think of the garden, Matilda?''

'It's lovely—I was looking at the little summer house.' She blushed, remembering the pure joy she had felt at the sound of the doctor's voice. 'I'd like one in our garden, for Father in the warm weather...'

Which started a pleasant discussion about gardens, and somehow this led to her life before she had come to live at Much Winterlow. The doctor, experienced in extracting information from reluctant patients, listened carefully, putting two and two together, no longer pretending to himself that he wasn't deeply interested and

aware at the same time that Matilda was going to be a
hard nut to crack...

After tea she went up to her room and got into her
pink dress, wondering uneasily if she had talked too
much. The doctor was being friendly and dining with
him would be delightful. But she mustn't forget that
probably he had been prevented in some way from going to Lucilla and was taking her out because he had
nothing better to do. He must be vexed at having to
waste his holiday...

She went back to the sitting room and he got up as
she went in.

'You look nice,' he said. He sounded like an elder
brother. 'If you're ready, we'll go.'

CHAPTER EIGHT

IN THE car Matilda said, 'You didn't bring Sam with you.'

'No; we went for a long walk and had a late lunch. He wouldn't take kindly to staying with Aunt Kate while we're away and I shall be home to take him for his evening walk.'

She had thought that maybe they were going to the hotel at Somerton but he drove through its main street and presently turned into a narrow country road. After a mile or so he turned in between stone pillars. There was no sign of a dwelling until he rounded a narrow bend, to reveal light from a dozen windows streaming towards them in the dark evening. As they reached it Matilda could see that it was a large house built in the Palladian manner. The doctor came to a silent halt before its imposing front door.

'Rather out of the way,' he observed, getting out and coming round to open her door, 'but I think you will like it.'

Matilda, thankful for the decent coat and the pink dress, said in her sensible voice, 'I would be out of my mind if I didn't. What a splendid house. I expect you've been here before.' and then she added, 'Sorry; that's none of my business.'

'If you mean have I brought Lucilla here, no, but I have brought my mother.'

Matilda paused on the steps leading to the entrance.

'I suppose that's what I did mean. It's the kind of place Lucilla would look right in; she is very lovely.'

'Quite beautiful,' the doctor agreed blandly as they went through the door.

She had often wondered what a country house hotel would be like; she had never expected to see one for herself. They had drinks in a lovely room with a blazing fire and presently went to the restaurant, softly lit with wide windows draped in old rose brocade and tables widely spaced.

Matilda, relieved to see that the rose-coloured dress stood up well to these surroundings, studied the menu.

'I hope you're hungry,' said the doctor—a remark she found encouraging. Vichyssoise, she decided—leek soup but with a difference—grilled trout with a pepper sauce, braised chicory and potato purée.

The doctor shared her wish for soup but settled on fillet of beef with sauce Perigord and turned his attention to the *maître d'* and the hovering wine waiter. Vintage claret for himself and a white burgundy for Matilda and, with the pudding trolley, champagne. Matilda, tucking into chestnut soufflé with chocolate sauce, enjoyed every mouthful, something which the doctor found endearing. Unlike Lucilla she appeared to have no qualms about weight problems. Her shape, he considered, was perfection itself.

The wine loosened her tongue nicely so that the sensible Miss Paige became Matilda—a Matilda he had fallen in love with—and who, most regrettably, showed no signs of falling in love with him.

He was prepared to wait just as he was prepared to tackle the problem of Lucilla. In the meantime he listened to Matilda's quiet voice and watched her happy face and possessed his soul in patience.

They sat a long time over their coffee and then he drove back to Aunt Kate's to find Mrs Chubb, cosy in a red dressing gown, waiting for them in the kitchen.

'Just in case you fancied a hot drink,' she told them. She looked at Matilda's happy face. 'Enjoyed ourselves, I'll be bound.'

'Yes, oh, yes!' said Matilda. She turned to the doctor, beaming up at him. 'Thank you very much for taking me out to dinner.' She sounded like a well-mannered child. 'It was a wonderful evening, you know—the kind of evening one always remembers…'

'Indeed, I shall always remember it too,' said the doctor. 'Sweet dreams, Matilda.' And he bent and kissed her, very much to Mrs Chubb's satisfaction and even more to Matilda's.

And, with a smiling glance at Mrs Chubb, he was gone.

Matilda turned a dreamy face to the housekeeper. 'I'll go to bed,' she said, and kissed her and floated upstairs to her room, for the moment wrapped in a dream world of her own.

But morning made short work of shattering dreams. She got up and showered and dressed and went downstairs to have breakfast with Aunt Kate, willing sensible thoughts to brush away the romantic nonsense of the previous evening. It's not as though he said anything, she told herself. We only talked about this and that; I could have been Aunt Kate or Mrs Chubb or a casual acquaintance. I hope I didn't talk too much…

'Where did you go?' asked Aunt Kate. 'And what did you eat?' Matilda told her at some length and her companion nodded briskly. 'Henry takes his mother there. She went there with his father when he was alive. They were a devoted couple. He has always said that

it was exactly the place in which to have a love affair...
And theirs was a love affair until his father died.'

She didn't give Matilda time to answer; 'We will go
to church this morning; you won't need to go home
until after lunch.'

The church, like so many in rural England, was too big
for the village; nevertheless it was well filled. And
Aunt Kate seemed to know everyone in it. Matilda sang
the hymns, said her prayers and listened to the sermon
carefully, anxious to dismiss her wandering thoughts,
and after some delay while Aunt Kate greeted friends
and acquaintances outside the church they walked back
to the cottage where Mrs Chubb was waiting to serve
roast beef with its traditional accompaniments.

'Mrs Chubb has the afternoon and evening off,' Aunt
Kate explained, 'so I have a cold supper.' She added
abruptly, 'I shall miss you and so will she.'

'I can never thank you enough for having me to stay.
You and Mrs Chubb are so kind and this is a lovely
cottage. I wish there was something I could do in return.'

'Bless the child.' Aunt Kate was at her most brisk.
'We enjoy your company and we hope that you will
come again and again to cheer up two old women.'

Matilda thought that neither Aunt Kate nor Mrs
Chubb needed cheering up; they appeared content with
their lot and satisfied with their lives. They shared so
many interests and they appeared to know everyone for
miles around. Matilda, eating the last of Mrs Chubb's
apple pie, wondered about the doctor's mother. Was
she as nice as Aunt Kate? Even half as nice...?

They had their coffee in the sitting room and presently Aunt Kate said, 'Go and get your hat and coat, Matilda; it's time you were going.'

Matilda put Taffy on the sofa and went upstairs. Now that it was time to go she wanted to go quickly and without fuss. She put on her hat and coat, gave a lingering look round the pretty room and went downstairs; Aunt Kate didn't approve of hanging about.

She was still sitting in her chair, her knitting in her lap, and leaning his vast person against the mantelpiece was Dr Lovell.

Matilda paused just inside the door. 'I'm just going,' she said stupidly.

'Then say goodbye and we'll be off.'

Aunt Kate said, 'Did I forget to tell you that Henry would drive you back? My memory is getting bad, I'm afraid.'

She put down her knitting and got to her feet. 'Now, child, you are not to work too hard and you must come again—after Christmas, for I'm sure you'll want to be home with your family and friends. Here's Mrs Chubb to say goodbye...'

Matilda was kissed and hugged while the doctor stood patiently waiting, then he kissed the two ladies and swept Matilda out to the car.

Sam was there, spread out on the back seat and pleased to see her. She submitted to his whiskery greeting and he rested his head on her shoulder, blowing gently into her neck.

'How very kind of you to take me home,' began Matilda.

'Sam fancied a drive. You have enjoyed your stay?'

'Oh, yes, very much. I hope you had a nice week.'

'It had its high spots. Mrs Inch will have tea ready— you'll stay? She will be so disappointed if you don't.'

'Oh, yes, please. I didn't tell Mother exactly when I would be home; Aunt Kate wasn't sure.'

'Good. Tomorrow morning after surgery I would like you to come out to Duckett's Farm. Rob is home and he would like to see you.'

'He's going to be all right? I'm so glad, and I'd like to see him and his wife and Tom.'

'Don't forget John.'

'What a lot of nice people there are—and you'd never meet them unless it was by chance.'

He agreed with a brief yes and she made no effort to talk any more, and before long she was being ushered into his house and Mrs Inch was welcoming her with as much warmth as Mrs Chubb.

'There's tea ready, sir; just you take Miss Matilda into the drawing room. Such a nasty cold afternoon; you'll be glad of a cup of tea and a slice of my lardy cake!'

The doctor was careful to keep the talk about nothing much as they ate their tea. Matilda's face had a happy glow which he could have watched for hours, but he had seen her quick glances at the long case clock behind him. She finished her tea and after a polite interval said that if he didn't mind she would like to go home.

His cheerfully brisk agreement was a bit disconcerting.

At the cottage she began on the thank-you speech she had rehearsed in her mind but he cut her short.

'I'll come in with you; I'd like a word with your father.'

Leaving Sam in the car, they trod up the path together and opened the door as Mrs Paige came into the hall.

'Matilda—oh, I'm so glad to have you back. I have

had the most wretched time with one of my heads; I was so tempted to ring and ask you to come home on Saturday morning but that would have been selfish. Now you are home I can take things easy.'

She turned to the doctor. 'So good of you to bring Matilda home. Do come in and forgive my bad manners. I get upset so easily.'

He watched the happy glow die away in Matilda's face. 'Thank you; I should like a word with Mr Paige.'

'Oh, I'm sure you will find him very well. He's in the sitting room.'

The doctor didn't stay long; a few minutes' quiet talk with Mr Paige, a courteous exchange of nothing much with Mrs Paige and he had gone, with a brief reminder to Matilda that he would see her at the surgery in the morning.

Mrs Paige complained that his visit had been so short. 'But I dare say he has more interesting things to do with his time; I suppose he felt obliged to bring you back, seeing as he suggested that you should go to his aunt's house in the first place.'

Mrs Paige sat down in the sitting room and picked up a book. 'Your father fancies something light for his supper—there's some soup and eggs...'

Matilda went up to her room. She always hoped that things would be different between her mother and herself but they never were. She went to the window and opened it, letting the cold air in, and then shut it again because Rastus, sleeping on her bed, protested.

It had been a lovely few days; she would remember them for the rest of her life and since there was no one else to tell she told Rastus of their delights.

She got the supper presently and listened to her mother making more plans. She had had another invitation, from old friends she had met while she had been away. 'Curry Rivel,' she explained. 'So handy for Taunton, I can do my shopping while I'm there. You'll let me have some extra money for Christmas, won't you? I'll get everything we shall need and bring it back with me.'

She looked sharply at Matilda. 'You'll have several days off at Christmas, I suppose?'

'I expect so. Dr Lovell will let me know.'

'Well, I plan to go at the end of the week and come back the day before Christmas Eve.'

'We shall be perfectly well here, my dear,' said Mr Paige. 'You go and see to the shopping and see the Gibbs; they have always been great friends of yours, haven't they? Perhaps in the New Year we might invite them back here. I do realise how lonely you are here; you had so many friends and were always so busy.' He sighed. 'I do so regret that I was forced to give up the ministry.'

'It's really nice living here,' said Matilda, 'and it will be lovely in the summer. I'll get the garden in some sort of order; it's full of plants and bushes, if only I could clear them.'

'A delightful prospect,' said her father, 'and so fortunate that you are so strong, my dear, for I am useless and your mother is far too delicate to undertake any but the lightest of tasks.'

Mrs Paige leaned across and patted his arm. 'You are so good to me...'

Matilda sat up late in her bed doing sums. She needed very little money for herself although she had hoped to buy a skirt and cardigan; now they would have to wait until after Christmas for she still had one or two more presents to buy. If she gave her mother most of her wages on Friday they should be enough to get the extra food and delicacies, the turkey and the Christmas pudding. She would talk to her mother in the morning.

The surgery was busy; with the holidays so near, everyone was intent on getting rid of their ailments as quickly as possible. Bidden to have coffee with the doctor afterwards, Matilda was told not to waste time. 'I've a long round this morning,' he explained, 'and I promised to go the Ducketts'. Can you be ready in ten minutes?'

She swallowed her coffee, got into her outdoor things and ran across the street to Mrs Simpkins' shop.

'I'm going to the Ducketts',' she explained breathlessly, 'and I must take something for little Tom.' she added, 'The doctor won't want to be kept waiting.'

Mrs Simpkins, rather in the manner of a conjuror with a rabbit in a hat, produced a small teddy bear sitting on top of a bag of sweets.

'Just the thing. Pay me later, love; he's getting into his car.'

Moments later he leaned over and opened the door for her and she scrambled in. Sam was in the back and heaved himself over to greet her with a pleased rumble, but the doctor didn't speak. She decided it was one of those days when she was Miss Paige, when it was better to be seen rather than heard.

And indeed he didn't speak until they arrived at the farm.

'Fifteen minutes,' he told her. 'I shall be most of the time with Rob but try and be ready.'

'Well really,' said Matilda coldly. 'When have I ever kept you waiting?'

He smiled but said nothing.

The Ducketts were waiting for them; she shook Rob's hand and told him how well he looked and was led away to the kitchen by Mrs Duckett and Tom. They had coffee and Tom had his teddy bear then John came in.

They were glad to see her again and there was so much to tell her about Rob. She sat with Tom on her lap and drank her coffee with one eye on the clock, and sure enough there was one minute of the fifteen left when the doctor joined them.

Everything was exactly as it should be, he told them; Rob would need to see his surgeon after Christmas and he was to take things very easy until then.

They all went out to the car then, calling Christmas good wishes as he drove out of the farmyard.

'I'll drop you in the village,' said the doctor, 'and see you at five o'clock.'

'Would you mind if I hung up one or two decorations in the waiting room?'

'Not in the least. Get whatever you want from Mrs Simpkins and tell her to put it on my bill.'

'I didn't mean you to pay for them.'

'Of course you didn't, but don't deprive me of that pleasure. I could never get Miss Brimble to do more than arrange a sprig of holly on her desk so let us be lavish.'

'Thank you; if you don't like it you'll say so?'

'Most certainly.'

He got out and opened her door and she turned to pat Sam. 'Thank you for taking me out to Duckett's Farm.'

'They wanted to see you.' He got into the car and

drove away. A perfectly sensible answer, she reflected, so why did she feel snubbed?

She had a wonderful time with Mrs Simpkins. Without the worry of having to pay for them, she chose Father Christmas in his sleigh for the table, several jolly Christmas scenes to hang on the walls, and yards of tinsel to fasten round the door. Holly, too, and a red paper shade for the ceiling light. She bore the lot back to the waiting room, let herself in and set about decorating it. It took time but she was pleased with the result. 'And if he doesn't like it it's just too bad,' she said.

She was late home, of course, and her mother was annoyed about that.

'We could have had a macaroni cheese if you had been here to make it.'

'I stayed to decorate the waiting room.'

'You never wasted your money on that?'

'No. Dr Lovell paid for everything.'

'I should hope so; he's rich enough. No wonder that Armstrong girl is anxious to marry him.'

The evening surgery was pretty busy and the doctor was late starting, but no one grumbled; they were too busy admiring the decorations. When he did come she didn't look at him as he opened the surgery door and called the first patient in, but when the last patient had gone and she was clearing up he came and stood in the centre of the room, his hands in his pockets.

'Very nice,' he commented. 'You've done us proud. And my patients loved it.' He stared down at her. 'But please don't attempt to decorate my surgery.'

He put out a hand and tucked a strand of hair behind her ear. 'Go home; you must be tired.' His voice was gentle.

Matilda, who had taught herself not to cry when she was still quite a small girl, swallowed back the tears. He was being kind, she reminded herself. It meant nothing more than that; she must look an object for his pity. The thought banished the tears and she said quite sharply, 'I am not in the least tired, Doctor. I'm glad you like the decorations.'

She got her coat and put it on. 'I'll see you tomorrow evening.'

He opened the door for her and wished her goodnight, locking the door after her, and then stood at the side window watching her walk down the street, her small back very straight and defiant.

It wasn't possible to avoid him for they saw each other every day but she retreated behind a businesslike manner if they needed to talk and found an excuse not to drink coffee with him after morning surgery.

The doctor, a man of no conceit, was at first puzzled and then resigned. He had every intention of marrying her; he would deal with problems as they arose but first he must wait with all the patience he could muster until she fell in love with him.

Mrs Paige, with most of Matilda's pay packet in her purse, left on Saturday morning, having begged a lift from Mrs Milton. She would be back on Monday, she promised, or Tuesday at the latest. With Christmas only a little more than a week away, she would be needed at home.

'I'll bring you some of that game pâté,' she promised her husband, 'from that delicatessen I told you about.'

They waved as she was driven away in Mrs Milton's car.

'Your dear mother, always so thoughtful of me,' said Mr Paige. Matilda took his arm as they went indoors. She agreed cheerfully because she loved him and her mother made him happy. The trouble is, reflected Matilda, making coffee for them both, they shouldn't have had me.

She went to the village presently and did the weekend shopping, and as she left the shop Lucilla Armstrong and her brother got out of a car and rang the doctor's bell. Her brother carried a weekend case. He turned and waved to Matilda but Lucilla ignored her.

'I hope he has a simply beastly weekend,' Matilda muttered as she went home. 'Oh, how could anyone love a person so horrid as Lucilla?'

There was no one to answer her. The cow leaning over the hedge looked sympathetic but what she really wanted was a shoulder to cry on, preferably the doctor's.

Lucilla and her brother were in church with the doctor on Sunday morning. Matilda wished them an unsmiling good morning, and went back with her father in Mrs Milton's car to cook their dinner.

Her father was quiet and she looked anxiously at him and felt relief when he remarked that he was missing her mother. 'But she will be home again tomorrow. We must make this a happy Christmas, our first in this cottage. I am happy here, my dear, and I believe that your mother will settle down just as happily once the winter is over.'

But there was a phone call while Matilda was at the surgery on Monday morning; her mother hadn't had time to do all her shopping. She would be home on Wednesday afternoon.

It was three o'clock on Wednesday morning when
Mr Paige had another heart attack. Matilda would never
know why she felt compelled to get out bed and cross
the landing to her parents' room. She found her father
ashen and sweating and only partly conscious. She
choked back her fright, found her voice and told him
not to worry, she was getting the doctor, and flew
downstairs to the phone.

'Lovell,' said his calm voice in her ear, and she
found her voice again.

'It's my father; he's having a heart attack. Do come
quickly.' she added, 'It's me, Matilda.'

'Five minutes. Leave the door open and go up and
reassure him.'

He came in quietly, large and reassuring and matter-
of-fact. He bent over Mr Paige and then opened his
bag.

'Go and get dressed, but first of all call an ambulance. Tell them that you are phoning for me and that
it is urgent.'

He turned back to the bed and she went to the phone
again and tore into her clothes. If her father had to stay
in hospital he would need a bag packed. She did that,
even remembering to put in his little bible and his fa-
vourite anthology of English verse. And by then the
ambulance was at the door and they were carrying her
father carefully down the stairs on a stretcher.

'I'll take you with me in the car,' said the doctor,
and she hurried to lock doors and windows and leave
food and water for Rastus. And all the while she didn't
allow herself to think.

She was there as they loaded the stretcher into the
ambulance, to peer into her father's unconscious face
and hold his hand for a moment; then, obedient to the

doctor's hand on her arm, she got into his car beside him.

Waiting for the ambulance to lead the way, she asked in a whisper, 'He'll be all right?'

'I can't tell you that, Matilda. It's a pretty massive heart attack, but once we get him to the hospital everything will be done. He is an excellent patient, quiet and unafraid and otherwise fit for his age. I wish I could tell you more but for the moment it is useless to speculate.'

At the hospital her father was taken to the intensive care unit. The doctor went with him, leaving her in the care of a young nurse in Casualty.

She was given a cup of tea and told kindly that once her father was in his bed she would be able to see him. So she sat quietly while nurses bustled to and fro and she tried not to think.

The doctor came for her after half an hour.

'Come and see your father,' he said, and he sounded very reassuring. 'He's rallied and is responding nicely to treatment. It's early days to say that he's out of the wood but at least we can see daylight through the trees.'

It was quite a long walk to ICU even if you counted the lifts from one floor to the next. And when they reached it she was put into a white gown several sizes too large and taken to her father's bed.

He was conscious and smiled a little as she bent to kiss him.

'Don't worry your mother.' His voice was faint but determined.

'In the morning I'll let her know that you are better,' she told him. 'She will want to know, Father, but I won't alarm her.'

'There's a good girl. Go home now and get some sleep.'

'Yes, Father. I'll come and see you later.'

She kissed him again and stood quietly while a nurse took her gown, and then made the endless journey to the entrance and got into the doctor's car again.

He fastened her seat belt. 'Don't come to surgery,' he told her. 'Go to bed and sleep. Come in the evening if you feel like it. I'll keep you posted about your father.' He glanced at his watch. 'It's almost six o'clock; you should ring your mother when you get home.'

'Yes, I'll do that. Her friends will bring her home. And if you don't mind I'd rather come to work. You see, if I'm busy, I don't think so much.'

'Just as you like.'

He took the key from her when they reached the cottage and went in with her, turned on the lights, put on the kettle and found the teapot.

'We both need a hot drink. I'll make tea while you phone your mother.'

It took a few minutes for Mrs Paige to be roused and fetched to the phone.

'In hospital? And Christmas only a few days away. Oh, dear, this is terrible news. I must go to him at once. Is he very ill? I was going out to lunch.'

'You'll come home today, Mother?'

'I can't think now, Matilda, I'm so upset. I'll phone you later.'

The doctor looked at her as she went into the kitchen. 'Your mother is upset? She will go straight to the hospital, will she not? And then come home. There are several people in the village who will willingly take her to see him whenever she wishes.'

He poured their tea, watching her pale face; she had

tied her hair back and her eyes looked huge. She
needed a warm bed and someone like Mrs Inch or Aunt
Kate to comfort her, but he was too wise to insist on
her not coming to the surgery in an hour's time.
Hopefully she would be so exhausted by the end of it
that she would go home to bed and her mother would
be there. Mrs Paige was a selfish, idle woman but she
was Matilda's mother...

He went away then with a casual, 'See you shortly,'
and she fed Rastus, had a bath and got dressed. There
wasn't much time for breakfast but in any case she
wasn't hungry; nonetheless she swallowed toast and
drank tea and then walked briskly to the surgery.

It was as busy as usual, full of people with minor
ailments and all very cheerful because it was
Christmas, and there was so much chatter that her unusual silence went unnoticed.

She was tired as the door shut for the last time. She
would hurry home and get a meal ready for her mother,
light the fire and ring the hospital.

The surgery door opened. 'I've rung the hospital.'
His arm swept her into the surgery and into a chair.
'He's making progress; that's good news.'

'Oh, I'm so glad. How soon will they know if he's
going to be quite well again? I mean to come home?'
She looked away. 'That's a silly question, isn't it?'

'No. A natural one. It may be ten days or more and
he will have to lead a careful life for a time.'

Mrs Inch came in then with coffee and a plate piled
high with hot buttered toast. 'You'll neither of you
have had breakfast,' she said severely, 'and you're to
eat every crumb.' She paused by Matilda. 'I'm that
sorry, Matilda. We're all hoping for good news.'

The doctor drove her home, saying that he had to pass the cottage anyway, but he didn't stay. Which was just as well as the phone rang as he drove away. Her mother.

'I've seen your father; he seems better. I won't come home; the Gibbs have persuaded me to stay with them. It will be so convenient for them to take me to the hospital each day. I'm terribly upset, of course, but everyone is being so kind. The doctors tell me that your father will have to remain in hospital for a week or ten days…'

'Over Christmas…'

'Yes. Of course I'd like to come home, Matilda, but you can understand that I must stay here so that I can see your father each day. You'll be all right? I dare say Mrs Milton will give you a lift if you ask her. I'll phone tomorrow; I must go now as we're going out to lunch.'

Matilda went into the kitchen, let Rastus out into the back garden and then went and sat down at the kitchen table. Of course her mother was very upset and there had been no time to discuss anything. Perhaps she would go to the Gibbs' and stay over Christmas with her mother? But what about Rastus? Or, if her father was out of danger, perhaps her mother would come home, just for Christmas, and hire a car to take them to the hospital on Christmas Day?

There was no point in worrying about it; first of all her father must recover. She went upstairs and made the bed up with clean linen and opened the windows. A few hours' sleep might be a good idea. She went downstairs and let Rastus in and then, with him for company, undressed and got into bed.

Her alarm clock woke her and she got up and showered and dressed and went to the kitchen to make herself a light meal. Later, after surgery hours, she would cook something. Then it was time for her to leave for the evening surgery but first she phoned the hospital. Her father was holding his own, she was told, and resting comfortably, and, yes, said the brisk voice at the other end of the phone, her love would be conveyed to the patient.

The doctor had a more detailed and reassuring message to give her when surgery was over. 'I won't bother you with all the technical details,' he told her. 'Your father is responding well but he will stay in ICU for the next day or two. You have heard from your mother?'

'Yes, she has been to see him and will go again tomorrow.'

'You are all right on your own until she returns home?'

'Yes. Yes, thanks, I'm fine.'

'I'll drive you to the hospital before surgery tomorrow. It will have to be early—six-thirty?'

'Six-thirty will be fine. Thank you.'

'Will your mother's friends bring her back home?'

'Yes, I'm sure they will...'

'Then why not give them a ring and get them to pick you up at the hospital? I expect your mother will be there.'

She said too quickly, 'Yes, of course I can do that. They're very old friends.'

'Good. I'll drive you home; get your coat.'

'There's no need. I always walk home...'

'But there is usually someone there when you get there. Come along.'

When they arrived he went into the cottage with her, turning on the lights, and as she went to the door with him he said, 'Phone me if you need me. Goodnight, Matilda.'

He didn't like leaving her there on her own, but her mother would be back tomorrow. He stood in the doorway looking down at her, small and matter-of-fact and independent. He bent and kissed her hard then went back to his car and drove away.

CHAPTER NINE

MATILDA, being a sensible girl, cooked herself some supper, had a bath, attended to Rastus and went to bed early, not sure if she would sleep. But she did, soundly, until her alarm clock woke her the next morning. The day was going to be a long one so breakfast had to be eaten in case she had to miss lunch, Rastus had to be seen to, the cottage locked up and what money she had stowed away in her handbag. The doctor hadn't said that he would pick her up so she locked the door and started down the path. She got to the gate as he drew up and got out. His good morning held a question.

'I was going to walk to the surgery,' she told him, not quite meeting his eye, the memory of his kiss very vivid in her mind. Perhaps he had forgotten it; his greeting had sounded businesslike.

He hadn't forgotten it; indeed, he wondered for one mad moment if he would kiss her again. But he didn't; he opened the car door for her and she got in, to be welcomed by Sam's pleased rumble.

The hospital's day was already under way. They went together to see her father and Matilda thought that he looked much better. He was pleased to see her. 'I shall be home again quite soon,' he assured her. 'Your mother spends much of each day with me. You are all right at the cottage?'

She assured him that she was and slipped away to allow the doctor to take her place. She waited quietly while he talked to the elderly doctor who had joined him and then went back with him to the car.

He took her back to the surgery, patiently answering her questions. Her father was making an excellent recovery but there was no question of him going home before Christmas.

'Your mother will be coming home today? There is no need for her to stay at the hospital each day.'

He wasn't looking at her so it was easier to assure him that she would be home very shortly. He said, 'Good. I know Mrs Milton will take either of you in at any time. Your father is out of danger and there is no reason why he shouldn't be perfectly well for years yet.'

He got out of the car, unlocked the door and went in with her. 'See you later,' he said, and, with a casual nod, disappeared into his room.

It was quiet and rather cold in the cottage, but there didn't seem much point in lighting the sitting-room fire. She went around the house, hoovering and dusting quite unnecessarily, until it was time to get her lunch. She sat at the kitchen table with Rastus beside her, eating scrambled eggs, fighting self-pity.

It was a dreary, cold day but there was plenty to do in the garden. In an old mac, her hair tied into a scarf, she worked until the early dusk, raking up dead twigs, leaves and all the debris of a neglected garden. She went indoors then, feeling better, glowing from the exercise, and made tea and phoned the hospital.

'A continued improvement,' said the voice at the other end, 'and your mother left a message for you. She will ring you tomorrow morning after you get home.'

It was a dark night and the cottage seemed forlorn and very empty. Supper and bed seemed a good idea. She wasn't a nervous girl but she couldn't help thinking of the empty fields between her and the village. Rastus, sensing her unease, crept close to her, and presently, lulled by his warmth and purr, she slept.

A few minutes after she had left the surgery the doctor had put down the phone. Lucilla had demanded that he should drive over to her home that evening.

'I don't want to spend Christmas at your house,' she had told him. 'I can't think why I ever agreed to it. Guy said I'd been a fool to agree. He's going to a hotel at Cheltenham with the Fergusons—remember them? He suggests we both join him there. I think it's a splendid idea…'

'Why don't you want to come here?'

'Oh, Henry, it'll be so dull—church and carols and just us and your mother and aunt and family. When we are married I intend to change your lifestyle—we might even move to Taunton or Cheltenham, or even Gloucester.'

'No,' the doctor had said.

'What do you mean, no? You don't intend to spend the rest of your life and mine in that old house?'

He'd said evenly, 'My family have spent their lives here for two hundred years or more; I intend to do the same.'

'Well, I don't.'

'If you wish to break our engagement I shall understand. I shan't change my mind, Lucilla.'

'Nor shall I, so you can forget that we were going to marry.'

She had slammed the receiver down and he'd sat for

a long time at his desk. Kindly fate had offered him a helping hand...

The next day, Matilda, with the plea of urgent shopping to be done as soon as surgery was over, gave him no chance to do more than bid her good morning. She spent some of her pay packet on groceries and went home. Perhaps her mother would change her mind now that her father was no longer in danger and come home.

But Mrs Paige had no intention of doing that. 'What would I do if I came home?' she wanted to know. 'Oh, I know someone would give me a lift in to the hospital if I asked, but you're not home much and I'd just sit in that cottage and be bored out of my mind.'

When Matilda didn't speak she added, 'Christmas would have been a very dull affair with just the two of us and I'm sure you'll find plenty to do. Everyone here is so kind, cheering me up, taking my mind off your father's illness. He'll be coming home soon, the doctor told me, and I've insisted that a nurse comes to attend him; I couldn't possibly manage. But you and she could do whatever has to be done.' And when Matilda still remained silent she said, 'You're still there? I hope you're not sulking?'

'No, Mother. I'm glad Father is so much better. Will you phone me tomorrow?'

'Yes, yes, of course.'

A good burst of tears helped. Matilda mopped her face, ate the lunch she didn't want and, although it was raining, went into the garden and started to clear the overgrown vegetable patch at the end of it.

Evening surgery over, the doctor came into the waiting room.

'I'll drive you back,' he told her. 'It's a wretched night.'

It's astonishing, reflected Matilda, how quickly one can think up a parcel of lies when desperate.

'Thank you, Doctor. But I'm going across to Mrs Simpkins' and Mr Simpkins will take me home later.'

She gave him a bright smile.

He looked at her thoughtfully. 'Your mother won't mind being alone?'

'Oh, no,' said Matilda airily. 'She doesn't mind at all and it's only for an hour or two.'

Rather mystified, he wished her goodnight and went to his study to work. He would go and see her in the morning, drive her somewhere quiet so that they could talk. He abandoned his writing and sat back in his chair, Sam at his feet, and allowed his thoughts to dwell on Matilda.

She was avoiding him, he was aware of that, but she hadn't drawn back when he had kissed her. And of course she thought that he and Lucilla were engaged. That they were meant for each other was so obvious to him that he had supposed that she must have been aware of that too.

He picked up his pen again and started to fill in forms and make notes. He was interrupted by Mrs Inch, who came in with such an air of urgency that he put his pen down again and asked what had upset her.

'There's something you should know, sir. Mrs Simpkins has just been over. Ben—the milkman, you know—went in for his groceries; she puts them aside for him. His brother works as a porter at the hospital...'

'Sit down, Mrs Inch. He saw or heard something, perhaps, this porter?'

'Indeed he did. That Mrs Paige—begging your par-

don, I'm sure—leaving our nice Matilda alone! He was
doing a job right by her when she was talking to one
of the sisters. She's staying with friends over
Christmas, not coming home, and that her daughter
would be with friends and her duty was by her husband, though this man heard one of the doctors telling
Mrs Paige that there was no need for her to be there
each day now. And there's that dear girl all alone, and
over Christmas too, and not said a word to anyone.'

Mrs Inch paused for breath. 'I'm that upset, sir. Not
that she'll be lonely; there'll be invitations enough
from half the village when they know and Mrs
Simpkins won't be slow to tell it around.'

The doctor was sitting back in his chair. 'Thank you
for telling me, Mrs Inch, and please tell Mrs Simpkins
that I shall go and fetch Matilda to stay here—now,
this evening. So would you delay dinner for half an
hour or so and get a room ready for her? The balcony
room at the back of the house, I think; we mustn't
forget Rastus.'

Mrs Inch blew her nose and mopped away a stray
tear. 'Oh, sir, I knew you would know what to do.' She
went to the door. 'We'll all be so pleased.'

The doctor's feelings were a good deal stronger than
pleasure but he gave no sign of his rage. He supposed
that since Mrs Paige was to be his mother-in-law he
would have to make an effort to like her; at the moment
he merely felt murderous towards her.

He went through the house and along the little pas-
sage which led to the garage, got into his car, and drove
away much too fast.

The kitchen window was at the side of the cottage;
he could see that the room was lit as he went up the
path and thumped the knocker.

He had to thump again before the hall light was switched on and Matilda's voice wanted to know who it was.

'Let me in,' roared the doctor, 'before I break the door down.'

Which he will surely do, thought Matilda, for my dearest Henry is in a bad temper. So she opened the door. He swept past her, taking her with him.

'How dare you,' he demanded. 'How dare you not tell me? Do you suppose that I would have left you alone for one minute if I had known? I must in time learn to like your mother but for the moment my feelings towards her are unmentionable...'

'You are extremely cross,' observed Matilda in a reasonable voice calculated to make him even crosser. 'Perhaps you will tell me why you are here?'

'Go upstairs and pack a bag. You're coming back to my house and don't argue about it; the entire village knows that's why I have come. Where do you keep the cat basket?'

Matilda said, 'On the bottom shelf of the cupboard by the sink.' And added, 'I won't pack a bag...'

'Please yourself; come as you are. Mrs Inch will have a nightie for you.'

He looked at her across the little room and smiled. 'This isn't the right time to tell you but Lucilla has decided not to marry me.'

'Well,' said Matilda, 'I have always known that she is most unsuitable for you but I can quite see why you fell in love with her. Are you unhappy?'

He said gravely, 'I am the happiest man on earth. Now go and pack that bag.'

So she did. And came downstairs again, looking

rather untidy. He took the bag from her and thought she was the most beautiful girl in the world.

He turned off the lights, shut the windows and, with Rastus in his basket, locked the cottage door behind them then popped her into the car. Matilda tried to think of something to say for his silence unnerved her. Her head teemed with snatches of poetry, first lines of hymns and nursery rhymes, none of which were any use as conversation. Perhaps it would be best to remain silent...

The doctor stopped outside his front door, got out to open the car door for her and, under the interested eyes gazing from neighbouring windows, ushered her into his house.

Mrs Inch came to meet them in the hall.

'There you are, Miss Matilda. Just you come with me; I'll take you to your room. Bring the little cat with you; there's a balcony—so handy for him.'

The doctor gave Matilda a little push and she followed Mrs Inch up the staircase, not speaking, only nodding when he said quietly, 'Come down again, Matilda, to the drawing room.'

The room was charming. Not overlarge but furnished with a brass bed covered by a patchwork quilt, a little tulip wood dressing table with a triple mirror, a bow-fronted chest of drawers and a delicate bedside table with a pink-shaded lamp on it. There were rose-pink curtains at the window and a door opening onto a small covered balcony.

'The bathroom is next door,' said Mrs Inch. 'Just you tidy yourself and come down to your dinner.'

So Matilda combed her hair and did things to her rather pale face and went back down the staircase, feel-

ing that she was in a dream and not at all sure what to
do next.

That was settled for her as she reached the hall. The
drawing-room door was opened and the doctor said,
'In here—have a drink before we have dinner.'

He sounded exactly the same as usual, as though her
sudden and unexpected arrival was all part of his day.

She took the chair he offered her and when he
handed her a glass of sherry tossed it down so that his
eyes widened with hidden laughter. But he refilled her
glass and sat down opposite her, Sam, as usual, at his
feet.

'I think,' said Matilda, much emboldened by the
sherry, 'that you must explain.' She frowned. 'No, perhaps I'd better explain.'

The doctor stretched his long legs and began to enjoy himself. 'Yes?'

'Well, I ought not to be here. I mean, I'm quite all
right at the cottage and it's so convenient that Mother
can stay with her friends and see Father each day, and
I quite see what she means; it would be very dull for
her to come home with just me—I mean, at Christmas
and all.' She paused. 'Of course I was a bit disappointed but it's a splendid idea.'

'It's nothing of the sort. It's a splendid arrangement
for your mother to enjoy Christmas with her friends.
Your father is now out of danger; there is no need to
visit him each day and he'll have all the care and attention he could possibly need.' He added gently, 'You
should have told me, Matilda.'

She took a sip—a large sip—of sherry. 'Well, I
would very much have liked to, only I couldn't, could
I? You'd have felt sorry for me...'

'I don't feel at all sorry for you despite the fact that I do know. Sorrow is not what I feel, Matilda.'

He took her empty glass from her. 'Here's Mrs Inch to tell us to come to dinner.'

There was soup—Mrs Inch's own version of French onion soup with cream on top and a circle of toasted bread—grilled salmon steaks with tiny new potatoes and salsify, and a mincemeat tart with clotted cream. And a white burgundy to go with it.

They didn't talk much; the doctor had a great deal to say but not yet, and Matilda, fed and warm and nicely vague from the sherry and the wine, was in no state to listen.

They had their coffee at the table and when they had drunk it he suggested that she might like an early night. Mrs Inch, waiting, as it were, in the wings, whisked her upstairs before she could say more than goodnight.

Someone had attended to Rastus's needs. Matilda had a quick bath and tumbled into bed and he joined her, pressed close to her side, smelling strongly of sardines. 'You had a good dinner too,' said Matilda sleepily, and closed her eyes.

In his study the doctor lifted the phone. 'Mother...' He talked at some length and then picked up the phone again and dialled Aunt Kate's number.

There was just one more problem. He looked up a number and dialled it. Having a bishop in the family could be useful...

At breakfast he was casually friendly, giving her no chance to utter her doubts and questions.

'I'll run you back to the cottage.' He saw with satisfaction the instant dismay on her face. 'You'll need a hat and coat if we're going to church.' It was the morning of the vicar's special pre-Christmas sermon, traditionally delivered on the last Saturday before Christmas.

'Very well. Thank you for having me, Dr Lovell; you have been very kind. Would you mind if Rastus comes with us? And my bag.'

'Yes, I do mind. Rastus stays here and so does your bag. I suggest that you pack a few more clothes while we're at the cottage.'

'Oh, but…'

'Darling girl, will you do as I ask?'

She stared across the table at him, the colour rushing into her face. 'Darling girl,' he said again, and smiled. 'And Henry is my name!'

'I can't…' she began, and stopped, not knowing how to go on.

'We had better go if you're finished; Mother and Aunt Kate will be here by the time we get back. They hadn't intended to come until Christmas Eve with the rest of the family—I think you will like my mother.'

'Christmas…' began Matilda.

'You are spending it at my house with my family—aunts and uncles, cousins—the house will be packed to the roof.'

'Mother…?'

'We will telephone her later. Your father is making excellent progress; he—and your mother—should be home before the New Year.'

Matilda felt that she was being swept away by a raging torrent, only raging wasn't quite the right word. Loving and caring were.

She went with him to the cottage and packed a case—the pink dress, woollies, a thick skirt, the grey jersey dress, undies, dressing gown and slippers. Was she to stay with the doctor until her parents came back? She didn't like to ask.

Mrs Lovell and Aunt Kate were placidly drinking coffee when they got back. They turned smiling, composed faces to them as they went into the drawing room. The doctor kissed them in turn. 'And here is Matilda,' he said to his mother, and stood back while that lady embraced Matilda.

There had been no need to be nervous, thought Matilda. This plump little lady had nothing but kindness in her elderly face.

'I've always wanted a daughter,' said Mrs Lovell, and beamed at her as Aunt Kate in her turn kissed Matilda.

Nothing is quite real, thought Matilda, sitting in the Lovells' pew, aware that the congregation were looking at her from under their hats. Mrs Lovell had said that she wanted a daughter but Henry hadn't said that he wanted a wife. She sat, not listening to a word of Mr Milton's sermon, fuming quietly, unaware that her hands were clenched tightly in her lap, until the doctor's large hand picked one up and held it fast. And when she peeped at him he smiled so that she glowed with happiness.

It took a long time to leave the church for so many people stopped to speak to them, talking trivialities, smiling and nodding to themselves as though they had discovered something interesting. Only Lady Truscott voiced the thoughts of the more discreet friends and acquaintances.

'Hear that Armstrong girl has thrown you over. Always thought your heart wasn't in it. But the best of luck this time, eh?'

She laughed heartily and tapped him on the arm, looking at Matilda, who, much to her annoyance, blushed.

Lunch was a cheerful meal; the talk was all of Christmas—the members of the family who would be coming, Christmas cards and presents—and how splendid it was that Mr Paige had recovered so well.

They had coffee in the drawing room and presently the doctor put down his cup. 'Matilda and I are going for a walk with Sam. Mrs Inch will bring the tea about four o'clock but we should be back by then.'

He turned to Matilda. 'Ready? You'll need some sensible shoes.'

She fetched the shoes, put on the coat and tied a scarf round her head. In the hall she said tartly, 'I wasn't asked if I wanted to go for a walk with you.'

He swung her round to face him. 'But you do, don't you? I didn't need to ask you because I know you so well—all of you: your thoughts and feelings, your kindness and delight in life. I'm not going to kiss you now or I shall be unable to stop. Come along.'

They went up the lane by the church, shrouded by trees, bare now, their leaves thick under foot. It was quiet and cold and the air was like wine. The trees thinned presently and the lane lay ahead of them, winding between wintry fields.

The doctor came to a halt and took Matilda in his arms.

'I fell in love with you a long time ago although I didn't know it at the time, and now I love you so deeply that I cannot go on without you, my darling. You are so beautiful…' He ran a gentle finger down her cheek. 'Will you marry me?' And then he added, 'No, don't answer yet; first this…'

He bent to kiss her and Matilda, who had often wondered what heaven was like, knew now that it was a lane between bare winter fields with Henry's arms around her. Presently she said, 'Yes, of course I'll marry you, Henry. I've been in love with you since the day you asked me if I would start work on Monday!'

She smiled up at him and was kissed once more. 'But it's all a bit difficult.' She went on, 'There's Father and Mother. They won't miss me very much but Mother isn't very happy cooking and doing housework and Father forgets to pay the bills.'

'Leave that to me, dear heart. When shall we marry? Don't, I beg of you, talk about June weddings; I'm not prepared to wait.'

'Well, I can't see just what to do—and I haven't any clothes…'

The doctor tightened his hold. 'My love, I said leave it to me. We'll have the banns read next Sunday. I'm prepared to wait a month but not a moment longer.' He kissed the tip of her nose. 'You may have all the clothes you want once we're married but you must be the loveliest bride the village has ever seen. I want the whole world to see you—the village, at least—I want the church full of friends and family, the organ and the choir and you coming towards me down the aisle with your father.'

Later, much later, they went back and found Mrs Lovell and Aunt Kate sitting over the remains of the tea tray.

'Matilda and I are to be married,' said the doctor.

Mrs Inch, coming in with fresh tea and more cakes, so far forgot herself as to say, 'I saw you going up the lane and I said to myself, He'll pop the question, and

I was right.' She arranged the tray just so. 'I'll just pop across and tell Mrs Simpkins; the village will be that glad…'

The doctor rang the hospital then. Mrs Paige would be in in the morning, he was told, and Mr Paige was sitting up in a chair.

'Then be kind enough to ask Mrs Paige to wait at the hospital until we come tomorrow morning, around eleven o'clock.'

'I'll still be your receptionist?' asked Matilda.

'Of course. Until I can find someone else. Mother, we intend to have a village wedding in a month's time.'

Mrs Lovell was unperturbed. 'Quite right, dear. A white wedding after the first dull weeks of January is just what we all need. Kate and I will be entirely at your disposal. Morning coats and wedding hats and a large reception?'

'Yes. As soon as the Paiges are back we can perhaps talk things over with them.'

Matilda said in her sensible voice, 'We couldn't possibly have a reception at the cottage.'

'I'm quite sure that Lady Truscott is longing to lend you her house,' said Aunt Kate. 'You have no need to worry about anything, Matilda.'

She went to bed that night with her head in a whirl, only certain of one thing: Henry loved her and they were to be married.

The next morning he drove her to Taunton. They went to the ward where her father was and found him in a chair and Mrs Paige walking to and fro impatiently.

'Dr Lovell, Matilda, I've been waiting for hours. Couldn't you have phoned?'

Matilda went to kiss her father and the doctor said nothing but went to greet his patient.

'You are to return home very shortly,' he said, 'and there is no reason why you shouldn't resume a quiet life again. We shall all be glad to see you back in the village.'

'Why do you want to see me?' asked her mother.

'Matilda and I are to be married.' He took Matilda's hand as he spoke and smiled at her. 'In a month's time at the village church. When you return home after Christmas you can discuss things with Matilda. She is, of course, staying with me. My mother and family are with me for Christmas.'

Her father was the first to speak. 'Matilda, my dear, what happy news. I am delighted for you both and wish you both every happiness.'

Mrs Paige said slowly, 'But how will I manage? I'm sure it's splendid news but you can't marry so soon. I must have help. Besides, there's no money for a wedding. You could have a very quiet one, of course.'

The doctor said blandly, 'We are having a big wedding; I have a large family and many friends and I want them all to come and see us married. As for the reception, I believe that Lady Truscott will have it at her house.'

'Oh, well, in that case—I must say I'm very surprised.'

Mrs Paige went to Matilda and kissed her cheek. 'At least you will be living near enough to see us frequently.'

'As to that,' said the doctor pleasantly, 'that may not be possible.' He turned to Mr Paige. 'Quite by chance an uncle of mine has asked me if I know of a scholar who would consider taking the post of curator of the ecclesiastical library and museum housed in a large country property near Cheltenham. There is a house with the job, a very fair salary and a fairly lively social life. I'm sure Mrs Paige could deal with that side of the job. It is a permanent position and they prefer an older man. I wondered if you would be interested? You would have plenty of leisure to continue your own writing.'

Mr Paige said slowly, 'It sounds a most promising offer. But will this recent illness be a deterrent?'

'Most unlikely. The work involved will be well within your capabilities.'

'Well, this is indeed a happy day for me. My dear, what do you think? Would you feel strong enough to undertake some social duties?'

Mrs Paige was smiling. 'Of course, my dear. It sounds ideal for you. When are you to go?'

The doctor said, 'I'll drive Mr Paige over after Christmas and if everything is satisfactory I imagine you can move there whenever it is convenient. But not before our wedding; you will want to help Matilda with that, will you not?'

Matilda listened to this in silence. Henry had told her not to worry, to leave everything to him, but all the same she had been worrying. And there had been no need; he was arranging everything exactly as he wanted it to be.

They went soon after, leaving a quietly contented Mr Paige and an excited Mrs Paige. Most of her excitement was at the idea of leaving the village but she spared a few thoughts about Matilda. She was going to lose someone who had always been on hand to help her, with money and time and a willing pair of hands; on the other hand dear Henry—he was already dear Henry—was well off and well connected. Very desirable in a son-in-law.

'You've made Father very happy,' said Matilda as they drove back. 'Do you suppose they'll accept him? It's exactly what he would like.'

'He'll be accepted, sweetheart. Have we any more problems?'

She had one—the wedding dress—but she wasn't going to bother him with that.

The next day it was work as usual. There would be a surgery tomorrow and then hopefully it would close down until after Boxing Day except for emergencies. The family would start to arrive tomorrow evening; Matilda inspected the pink dress and hoped that it would do, and while she was doing that Mrs Inch came to see her.

'I dare say you've got plans of your own, miss. But you might like to know that Mrs Vickery—she dressmakes, you know—has a length of white silk crêpe going begging. A customer decided not to use it and Mrs Vickery bought it off her. She was wondering if you'd like her to make you a wedding dress from it? She makes nicely…'

'Mrs Inch, that's exactly what I would like. Could I go and see her after Christmas? Would you tell her if you see her? I'll go the day after Boxing Day.'

There was another small problem: she had some presents but still nothing for Henry and his mother. She nipped across to Mrs Simpkins', who, full of enthusiasm at the turn of events, delved into various boxes and drawers. She had a little water colour of the village,

painted by a visiting artist and put away ready for the
tourists in the summer, and a silver pencil which
Matilda thought Henry might never use; but there was
nothing else...

It was Christmas Eve, and the family had all arrived
by now—pleased to see each other, delighted to meet
Matilda and make much of her. Going down in the pink
dress for dinner, she found the doctor waiting for her.

The hall was empty and he held her close and kissed
her. 'Come into the study; I've something for you.'

A ring: sapphires in an old-fashioned gold setting.
He slipped it onto her finger. 'It was my grandmother's;
she left it to me to give to my bride.'

Matilda said, 'It fits and it's beautiful. Thank you,
Henry.' And she thanked him suitably, which meant
that she had to tidy her hair before they went to join
everyone else.

And Christmas Day was a day never to be forgotten.
Everyone went to church, even Mrs Inch and Kitty,
although Mrs Inch did slip off halfway through the service to baste the turkey. And there was coffee for anyone who wanted it after the service, although the doctor
left his mother to act as hostess while he drove Matilda
to the hospital. She sat close to him and Sam had his
head pressed against her. She was almost too happy to
talk.

Mr Paige looked to be almost his old self and Mrs
Paige, with the prospect of a future more to her liking,
was prepared to like everyone. Her friends were coming for her presently; she told Matilda that she would
stay until Mr Paige had had his Christmas dinner.

The doctor had left them briefly and when he returned it was to tell them that Mr Paige could go home in a week.

'I must pull myself together,' said Mrs Paige, 'for there will be a great deal to do if you are determined to marry so soon.'

The doctor was a splendid host. Nothing had been overlooked: there was a tree, presents, a magnificent dinner table, champagne. Matilda, sitting beside him as he carved the turkey, wondered how he had found time to plan it all. She caught his eye and they smiled at each other—two people very much in love.

They had just finished breakfast on Boxing Day when the doctor was called to a small farm some miles from the village. One of the boys in the family had cut himself badly.

'I'll come with you,' said Matilda.

It wasn't very serious, only needing a few stitches, an injection and instructions to go to the surgery in a few days' time. They stopped in a lay-by to talk on the way back.

'I shall have to go home to get ready for Mother and Father.' She tucked a hand in his. 'I can go on working for you?'

'Yes, until I can find someone to take over. And you have no need to go home until the day before their return.'

'But Mother will want to start packing up...'

'They won't move until after our wedding and I've no doubt that there will be some help available.'

So she stayed at his house and part of the day she was Miss Paige in the waiting room and part of the day she was Matilda in her future home.

But she was home to welcome her parents and almost the first thing her mother said was, 'Your wedding dress, Matilda; you had better hire it—there's a shop in Taunton.'

Mrs Vickery was making a splendid job of the white silk crêpe. Matilda said, 'There's no need, Mother. I have my dress.'

'Well, really; am I to have no say in the matter?'

A question which Matilda prudently didn't answer.

The year was a month old. It was a still day with the pale sun shining on early morning frost. Matilda got up early, made tea, got the breakfast and found her father's spectacles and zipped her mother into her dress, then she went to her room.

She took her wedding dress from the empty wardrobe and put it on, fastened the little buttons on its long sleeves, fastened Henry's pearls around the modest neckline and then sat down to arrange her veil before the mirror. A simple one lent to her by his mother.

When her mother came in, she was standing by the open window listening to the church bells already ringing.

Mrs Paige stopped short at the door. 'Matilda—why, you look so pretty.' And just for a moment she forgot to be selfish and thoughtless. 'I hope you will both be very happy.'

Matilda kissed her mother's cheek. 'We shall be, Mother. We love each other.'

The drive to church with her father in the beribboned car was short. There was a small crowd outside the church gates, calling out to her and wishing her well, and in the porch the two small bridesmaids, Henry's nieces, waited. Through the open door she glimpsed a packed church. Henry had told her that he wanted the whole world to see them wed and he had achieved his wish; the village had turned out to a man, mingling with his family and friends.

She saw grey waistcoats and top hats in the pews, splendid creations on the ladies' heads, early spring flowers, old Miss Clarke thumping away at the organ and the choir ready to burst into 'The Voice that Breathed o'er Eden'. Not one single embellishment of their day had been forgotten.

Miss Clarke allowed the organ to dwindle to a few soft notes and the choir opened their mouths as the congregation rose to its feet, every head turned to see the bride. All except Henry.

Matilda tweaked her father's sleeve and they started down the aisle. When they were almost at the altar steps the doctor looked round. And such was the look of love on his face that she wanted to break into a run and feel his arms around her. But she didn't; she paced slowly to his side and smiled up at him as he took her hand in his.

Mr Milton opened his prayer book. He began, 'Dearly beloved, we are gathered together here...'

For Matilda's wedding...!

Harlequin Romance®

**On their very special day,
these brides and grooms are determined
the bride should wear white...
which means keeping passion in check!**

True love is worth waiting for...

Enjoy these brand-new stories from
your favorite authors

MATILDA'S WEDDING (HR #3601)
by **Betty Neels**
April 2000

THE FAITHFUL BRIDE
by **Rebecca Winters**
Coming in 2000

Available at your favorite retail outlet, only from

HARLEQUIN®
Makes any time special.™

Visit us at www.romance.net

HRWW2

If you enjoyed what you just read,
then we've got an offer you can't resist!

Take 2 bestselling
love stories FREE!

Plus get a FREE surprise gift!

Clip this page and mail it to Harlequin Reader Service®

IN U.S.A.	**IN CANADA**
3010 Walden Ave.	P.O. Box 609
P.O. Box 1867	Fort Erie, Ontario
Buffalo, N.Y. 14240-1867	L2A 5X3

YES! Please send me 2 free Harlequin Romance® novels and my free surprise gift. Then send me 6 brand-new novels every month, which I will receive months before they're available in stores. In the U.S.A., bill me at the bargain price of $2.90 plus 25¢ delivery per book and applicable sales tax, if any*. In Canada, bill me at the bargain price of $3.34 plus 25¢ delivery per book and applicable taxes**. That's the complete price and a savings of 10% off the cover prices—what a great deal! I understand that accepting the 2 free books and gift places me under no obligation ever to buy any books. I can always return a shipment and cancel at any time. Even if I never buy another book from Harlequin, the 2 free books and gift are mine to keep forever. So why not take us up on our invitation. You'll be glad you did!

116 HEN CNEP
316 HEN CNEQ

Name	(PLEASE PRINT)	
Address	Apt.#	
City	State/Prov.	Zip/Postal Code

* Terms and prices subject to change without notice. Sales tax applicable in N.Y.
** Canadian residents will be charged applicable provincial taxes and GST.
   All orders subject to approval. Offer limited to one per household.
   ® are registered trademarks of Harlequin Enterprises Limited.

HROM00   ©1998 Harlequin Enterprises Limited

Back by popular demand are

DEBBIE MACOMBER's

Hard Luck, Alaska, is a
town that needs women!
And the O'Halloran brothers
are just the fellows
to fly them in.

Starting in March 2000 this beloved series returns
in special 2-in-1 collector's editions:

MAIL-ORDER MARRIAGES, featuring
Brides for Brothers and *The Marriage Risk*
On sale March 2000

FAMILY MEN, featuring
Daddy's Little Helper and *Because of the Baby*
On sale July 2000

THE LAST TWO BACHELORS, featuring
Falling for Him and *Ending in Marriage*
On sale August 2000

Collect and enjoy each MIDNIGHT SONS story!

Available at your favorite retail outlet.

HARLEQUIN®
Makes any time special ™

Visit us at www.romance.net

PHMS